"You n̶ what rebellious, unseemly fantasies occasionally rush through my head,"

Tyler said softly. Immediately he felt an increase in Samantha's pulse. The knowledge that his words had somehow stimulated her aroused a dangerous fever.

He released her wrist and drew a steadying breath. "However, I pick and choose my rebellions very carefully, and I know fantasies are best left as unfulfilled illusions."

"Now that's where you're wrong, Tyler," Samantha replied, her voice husky and low. "Some fantasies make wonderful reality. You just have to know which ones to reach out for and which ones to leave alone...."

Dear Reader,

Everyone loves Linda Turner, and it's easy to see why, when she writes books like this month's lead title. *The Proposal* is the latest in her fabulous miniseries, THE LONE STAR SOCIAL CLUB. Things take a turn for the sexy when a straitlaced lady judge finds herself on the receiving end of an irresistible lawyer's charms as he tries to argue her into his bed. The verdict? Guilty—of love in the first degree.

We've got another miniseries, too: Carla Cassidy's duet called SISTERS. You'll enjoy *Reluctant Wife*, and you'll be eagerly awaiting its sequel, *Reluctant Dad*, coming next month. Reader favorite Marilyn Pappano is back with *The Overnight Alibi*, a suspenseful tale of a man framed for murder. Only one person can save him: the flame-haired beauty who spent the night in question in his bed. But where is she? And once he finds her, what is she hiding? Brittany Young joins us after writing twenty-six books for Silhouette Romance and Special Edition. *The Ice Man*, her debut for the line, will leave you eager for her next appearance. Nancy Gideon is back with *Let Me Call You Sweetheart*, a tale of small-town scandals and hot-running passion. And finally, welcome first-time author Monica McLean. *Cinderella Bride* is a fabulous marriage-of-convenience story, a wonderful showcase for this fine new author's talents.

And after you read all six books, be sure to come back next month, because it's celebration time! Intimate Moments will bring you three months' worth of extra-special books with an extra-special look in honor of our fifteenth anniversary. Don't miss the excitement.

Leslie Wainger

Leslie J. Wainger
Senior Editor and Editorial Coordinator

Please address questions and book requests to:
Silhouette Reader Service
U.S.: 3010 Walden Ave., P.O. Box 1325, Buffalo, NY 14269
Canadian: P.O. Box 609, Fort Erie, Ont. L2A 5X3

RELUCTANT WIFE

CARLA CASSIDY

Published by Silhouette Books

America's Publisher of Contemporary Romance

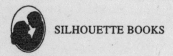

SILHOUETTE BOOKS

ISBN 0-373-07850-1

RELUCTANT WIFE

Copyright © 1998 by Carla Bracale

Printed in U.S.A.

Books by Carla Cassidy

Silhouette Intimate Moments

One of the Good Guys #531
Try To Remember #560
Fugitive Father #604
Behind Closed Doors #778
†*Reluctant Wife* #850

Silhouette Romance

Patchwork Family #818
Whatever Alex Wants... #856
Fire and Spice #884
Homespun Hearts #905
Golden Girl #924
Something New #942
Pixie Dust #958
The Littlest Matchmaker #978
The Marriage Scheme #996
Anything for Danny #1048
*Deputy Daddy #1141
*Mom in the Making #1147
*An Impromptu Proposal #1152
*Daddy on the Run #1158
Pregnant with His Child... #1259

*The Baker Brood
†Sisters

Silhouette Desire

A Fleeting Moment #784
Under the Boardwalk #882

Silhouette Shadows

Swamp Secrets #4
Heart of the Beast #11
Silent Screams #25
Mystery Child #61

Silhouette Books

Shadows Short Story 1993
"Devil and the Deep Blue Sea"

The Loop

Getting it Right: Jessica

Yours Truly

Pop Goes the Question

CARLA CASSIDY

had her first Silhouette novel, *Patchwork Family*, published in September of 1991, and since that time she has written over twenty-five books for five Silhouette lines. She's looking forward to writing many more books and bringing hours of pleasure to her readers.

Chapter 1

The second most difficult thing Samantha Dark had ever done was return to her hometown of Wilford, Kansas. The *most* difficult had been six years ago, when she had left. No, not left. *Run,* she amended, as she pulled her car into a parking space in front of the local coffee shop. At the age of twenty-three, she'd run away from her family, leaving this small town behind.

Now she was back, but she was reluctant to go directly to the big house where nobody awaited her. Where no welcome would warm her.

She checked her watch. It was after seven. She might as well get a bite to eat before continuing on to the house. As she got out of her car she saw the figure of an older man walking away from the coffee shop, the limp in his gait instantly recognizable.

"Jeb?"

He paused and turned, his wrinkled face wreathing in a smile as he recognized her. "Samantha? Samantha

Dark?'' He hurried toward her, his limp more pro-
nounced with his rapid steps.

Affection welled up inside her as the man gave her
a hug, then stepped back. He grinned; his warm,
crooked smile had always had the magic to make Samantha feel better, no matter how miserable she was.
"When did you get back in town?" he asked.

"Just this moment. I haven't even been to the house
yet." She took his hand in hers. "You're the first person
I've seen since driving into town. Tell me, are you still
caretaking at the cemetery?"

He nodded. "Where else would I be? That's the one
place the patrons don't complain much. I do my job,
supervise the grounds and keep the kids out."

"You never kept me out," Samantha reminded. She
released his hand, remembering all the times the cemetery and old Jeb had calmed her, consoled her. She had
often run there when her father had been harsh, knowing Jeb would wipe away the tears and soothe her
wounded heart.

The first time she'd met Jeb she'd been hiding behind
a headstone, sobbing out her unhappiness. Jeb had
found her, consoled her and that had been the beginning
of a special friendship.

He grinned. "You were a special case." He averted
his gaze and his smile faltered. "Samantha, I'm glad to
see you because I've got trouble. Maybe you can help."

"What? What's wrong? You know I'll do whatever
I can."

"It's not me. It's my boy."

"Dominic? What's wrong with him?" A mental vision of Dominic Marcola in his uniform came to mind
instantly. Dark hair and eyes, a good-looking man a
couple of years younger than Samantha.

"He was arrested yesterday."

"What?"

Before her eyes, Jeb seemed to age. The lines in his face appeared to deepen with his expression of helpless grief. "He was arrested. For murder."

Samantha started in surprise as the word hung ominously in the evening air. When she left Wilford six years ago, Dominic had just gotten a job on the police force.

"They say he killed Abigail Monroe, but my boy wouldn't hurt anyone. Somebody is setting him up to take a fall and he needs your help."

"My help?"

Jeb took one of her hands in his. "Please, talk to Mr. Sinclair. He worked for your father. He'll listen to you. Ask him to take Dominic's case. We aren't wealthy people, but I'll do whatever it takes to see my boy gets the best, and Tyler Sinclair is the best defense lawyer in the state of Kansas." He squeezed Samantha's hand. "Please, talk to him."

The last thing she wanted to do was ask a favor from Tyler, but she couldn't forget how Jeb had always been there for her, drying her tears, buoying her spirits, soothing the damage her father's cruel words had done. "I'll talk to him and see what I can do," she agreed. Gratefully he squeezed her hand, then released it.

"I'm sorry about your father," he added.

Samantha nodded, unsure how to reply. She was sorry, too.

About a lot of things. She was sorry her father had passed away two weeks ago, and she hadn't even known about it until yesterday. She was sorry he hadn't known how completely she'd turned her life around.

Most of all she was sorry she hadn't been able to tell him she loved him.

As yet, she simply hadn't had enough time to digest the fact of her father's death. She didn't even know how he'd died—whether he'd been ill or if it had been some sort of accident.

"I've got to get to work," Jeb said, pulling Samantha from her thoughts. "You'll let me know about Tyler as soon as possible?"

"Of course," she replied.

"I'm glad you're back, Samantha. It's past time you came back here where you belong." With a tired smile, he turned and limped away.

"Back where you belong." His parting words echoed in her head as she watched him leave. The problem was she wasn't certain exactly where she belonged.

She had run from here, seeking happiness in distant places, amid strangers. It hadn't worked. Somehow she'd known all along that her happiness would eventually be tied to this place, and to exorcising the personal demons that had driven her away.

She got back into her car, realizing all thoughts of hunger had fled with Jeb's plea for help. Although the idea of facing Tyler Sinclair was repugnant, it would have to be done sooner or later. She supposed it might as well be now.

Tyler Sinclair. When Tyler was seventeen years old, Samantha's father, Jamison Jackson Dark, had taken the boy under his wing. Tyler had become the son Jamison never had, and Jamison had directed all of his affection, all of his praise on the darkly handsome young man Samantha had grown to despise.

If Tyler ran true to form, the odds were good he would still be at the office. Of course, just because he'd been a workaholic six years ago didn't mean things hadn't changed.

A tiny flicker of triumph flared inside her as she pulled up in front of her father's law office and saw a light burning on the second floor. She'd been right. Tyler was here.

Samantha parked the car but remained sitting, gathering her courage to go inside. She pulled her keys from the ignition and found the one that would open the front door of the two-story building. She wondered vaguely if her father had changed the locks. She doubted it. Jamison had thrived on the very sameness of his life. He'd orchestrated it to provide a rigid methodical predictability that had driven Samantha crazy.

The building was gray brick with wood accents. It was impressive, radiating a dignity out of place amid the other storefronts. Samantha's entire life, until the time she'd left Wilford, had revolved around this place.

Her father had not only worked here, he'd also guided his two daughters' lives from here, laying down family rules and dispensing discipline from behind his massive oak desk. Samantha remembered one year when he'd been so involved in a sticky case, they'd celebrated Christmas in his office.

Samantha had always loved this building. She loved the smell of paper and ink, the aroma of coffee warmed too long and the lingering scent of fast food from working lunches. All the odors together combined in her mind to form what was to her the scent of justice.

She finally got out of her car and walked toward the front entrance. The large copper plaque above the door announced the establishment. Justice Inc. Jamison Jackson Dark: Senior Partner. The latter had always amused

Samantha. Senior partner? Her father had been the *only* partner.

The key worked. She pushed the door open and stepped inside, careful to lock the door behind her. Silence greeted her. The lobby was small, but tastefully furnished in shades of rich burgundy and forest green.

Nothing appeared to have changed. Except now her father was dead. She couldn't believe he'd passed away and neither Tyler nor her sister, Melissa, had contacted her. She shoved aside this thought, refusing to be ambushed by any unexpected grief. She needed all her wits about her to deal with Tyler.

Her father's office was on the first floor at the back of the building, but Samantha didn't go there. Instead she headed for the stairway.

As she climbed the steps, her mind filled with a vision of Jeb's face—the worry lines on his forehead, the deep grief that shadowed his eyes. He'd had the look of hopeless fear that she recalled seeing in the eyes of many of her father's clients.

The idea of Dominic murdering anyone was absurd. She remembered him as an intense, sober young man who had aspired to be a police officer since he was a child. Samantha had attended the ceremony inducting him into the force and would never forget the pride on his face, and on his father's.

Jeb was right about one thing. Tyler Sinclair was not only the best defense lawyer in the state of Kansas, he was probably the best west of the Mississippi. For now. The words shimmered in her head like a golden promise. Eventually, she intended to give him a run for his money.

His office door was closed, but she could hear the faint sounds of life emanating from within. The shuffle of papers. The creak of a chair. Even through the door she imagined she could feel his energy. Powerful. Vibrant. Arrogant.

She narrowed her eyes, irritated by her fanciful notions. Drawing a deep breath, she opened the door and stepped into his office. He sat at the desk facing her. At the sight of her, he leaned back in his chair and smiled. "Hello, Samantha. I've been expecting you for the last two weeks."

Immediate irritation reared up inside her. "That's strange. How could you be expecting me when you didn't even bother to let me know Father had died?"

He reached into his top drawer, withdrew a handful of letters and tossed them on the top of his desk. Samantha took a step closer, close enough to see that the letters were addressed to her at her old address and had been stamped return to sender. She felt the heat of color flush her face. "I moved. I guess the forwarding change of address expired."

"That makes it difficult to get in touch with you." He gestured toward the chair in front of his desk. "Please. We have some things to discuss."

Although she would have preferred to stand, feeling as though she needed the advantage of being taller than him while he sat, she moved to the chair and sat down.

"Just give me a moment," Tyler said and directed his attention back to some paperwork in front of him. As he made notations on the top sheet of a legal pad, Samantha took the opportunity to study him.

Six years hadn't changed him except to enhance his features, making him more handsome than ever. He'd been twenty-six years old when she left. That made him thirty-two now.

There was no sign of gray in his thick, styled, black

hair, and the lines that radiated like starbursts at the corners of his eyes only added character. Despite the lateness of the hour and the fact that he was alone, he still wore his suit jacket, with tie neatly in place. He looked as fresh and vibrant as he probably had when he left for work this morning.

Samantha was aware that her long day showed in the wrinkles of her dress and the messy escape of hair from her braid. She'd worn her lipstick off long before noon and hadn't replaced it, and she suspected her mascara had smudged dark shadows beneath her eyes.

Tyler had always made her feel this way—unkempt and inadequate. Samantha straightened her back, reminding herself she was no longer the out-of-control twenty-three-year-old she'd been when she left here. She was twenty-nine, had completed law school with grades in the top-ten percentile, and she wasn't about to be intimidated by the shrewd, handsome man in front of her.

"There." He set down his pen and closed the manila file he'd been working on. Once again he leaned back in his chair, his gaze so blue, so direct, but with a touch of amusement that made her want to scream. "Since we couldn't contact you to tell you about Jamison's death, how did you find out?"

"I have a subscription to the Wilford *Sun.* Unfortunately I don't read it every day. Yesterday I was doing a little catching up and found his obituary."

The humor left his eyes. "I'm sorry you had to hear about it that way."

She shrugged. "It's my own fault. I didn't think about the forwarding address expiring, and my phone number was unlisted." It was also her own fault for intentionally staying so out of touch with everything and everyone in Wilford. Remorse shot through her at this thought. She laced her hands together in her lap, wanting to look as cool and composed as he did. "How did he die?" Her voice cracked slightly with strain, belying the aura she'd tried to maintain.

"An accident. He fell from the balcony in your mother's bedroom."

Samantha stared at him. It was the same way her mother had died when Samantha was six years old. "That's impossible," she replied in a whisper. "Father hadn't been in her room for over twenty years—not since she died. He certainly would never have gone onto that balcony. He was scared of heights."

Tyler shrugged. "The facts speak for themselves. He was found the next morning on the terrace. The railing on the balcony was old and rotten. Apparently it broke away and he fell."

It wasn't right. Something about it just wasn't right. Samantha felt it in her gut but didn't know what to do about it.

Tyler leaned forward, and Samantha caught a wave of his scent. Spicy cologne mingled with clean soap; a pleasant scent that caused a memory to flood Samantha's mind.

She remembered cuddling against him in the dark interior of a car, her hand caressing the firmness of his thigh. That same scent had surrounded her then, and despite the numbing effects of the alcohol she'd consumed, she'd been filled with the desire to hold and be held by him.

She snapped back to the present, refusing to allow the memory to go any further, not wanting to relive one of her greatest humiliations—the night she had tried to seduce the great Tyler Sinclair.

"Your father left behind a will," Tyler said. "According to the terms, you and Melissa each get half of the house and its contents. I've been living there since Melissa got married, but I'll make arrangements to move out immediately if you intend to stay in town."

"I intend to stay here, but you don't have to move out. It's a big house and there's really no point in making any changes until I talk to Melissa and we decide what we're going to do."

She rubbed her forehead, feeling as if she was being assaulted by too much information. "When did Melissa get married?" So much time, so many events had been missed because of her own stubbornness and pride. Her heart suddenly ached with the need to see her sister.

"She married about six months after you left town, but she and her husband recently separated."

"Did she marry anyone I know?"

Tyler shook his head. "I don't think so. His name is Bill Newman. He moved here soon after you left. He runs a heating-and-cooling business."

Again Samantha touched her forehead, realizing a headache was attempting to gain hold. "I can't believe I allowed myself to get so out of touch," she said with a tinge of regret.

"As I recall, your parting words when you left here were that you never wanted to see, think of, or talk to anyone from the town of Wilford for the rest of your life," Tyler reminded her wryly.

"And there are still some people I feel that way about," she replied coolly, hoping he realized in no uncertain terms that he was one of those people. "But I've grown up considerably in the years I've been away and understand sometimes it's necessary to deal with people you don't particularly like."

Once again, a flicker of humor filled his eyes. "I'm glad you feel that way, because it looks like you and I will have to deal with each other in the future."

"Why? What are you talking about?" she asked.

"Your father's will made provisions for the firm. Fifty percent of it goes to you and fifty percent of it goes to me."

"Congratulations," she said sarcastically. "I guess sucking up to my father for all those years finally paid off."

This time his eyes flickered with a darker emotion—anger and perhaps a tinge of hurt. That surprised her. She'd never seen him express anything close to hurt before. He stood and walked to the window, his broad back toward her. She cursed herself for the childish barb. What was it about him that always brought out the worst in her?

"I know you don't believe me, Samantha, but I cared about your father. I never gave a damn about his money." He turned and eyed her, his features once again carefully devoid of emotion. "I'll make a fair offer to buy you out."

"That's funny. I was just about to say the same thing," she replied.

For a moment they faced each other, equal partners, but apparently neither of them interested in a partnership venture. How could a man who looked so hot be so cool? Samantha wondered. His rigid self-control was one of the things about him that had always driven her crazy. Just once, she would love to see him lose control, go a little crazy. Samantha knew all about going a little crazy.

"What about Melissa? Didn't Father leave her any part of the firm?" she asked.

Tyler shook his head. "He left her a generous trust fund instead."

Samantha stood, not wanting him towering over her, and changed the subject. "I stopped by the coffee shop a little while ago and ran into Jeb Marcola. He wants you to represent Dominic."

"I know. He's called me about a dozen times since Dominic was arrested."

"Are you going to take the case?"

He shook his head. "It's a loser. From what I've heard, the circumstantial evidence is overwhelming, as is the forensic evidence."

"Ah, now I understand how you got your reputation for winning. You only try the easy cases."

Again his eyes darkened but his mouth curved into a humorless smile. "A good lawyer takes cases on gut instinct. My instincts tell me this is one to stay away from."

"But I know Dominic. I'm sure he didn't kill anyone."

Tyler stepped around the desk and came to stand right in front of her. "You *knew* Dominic. You've been gone for six years, Samantha. Things happen. People change."

"People don't change that much. Dominic isn't a killer."

"As usual, you're not thinking with your head. You're thinking with your heart."

She stepped back, her heart thudding an unnatural rhythm at his closeness. "I'm surprised you'd recognize that, seeing as you don't have a heart."

He laughed and moved back behind his desk. "A good lawyer doesn't have to have a heart." He sat down. "In fact, most lawyers would consider the possession of a heart a liability."

Samantha eyed him narrowly. Her father had taught
him well. It was the kind of cold, harsh philosophy Jamison Jackson Dark would have spouted. "So you
won't represent him?"

"It isn't a case I want. It's going to be a high-profile
nightmare. This firm has always been conservative,
steering clear of controversial, publicity-laden cases."

Samantha drew a deep breath as she remembered the
look on Jeb's face. She had to help him…help Dominic.
Jeb had always been there for her. "I now own fifty
percent of this law firm?" she asked.

Tyler gazed at her in speculation and nodded slowly.
"Samantha, Justice Inc. doesn't take cases like Dominic's."

"It does now." She smiled and withdrew a copy of
her law degree from her purse. She tossed it on his desk.
"If you won't represent him, then I will. See you later,
partner." She walked out of his office, his shocked expression engraved in her mind.

It was only when she got back into her car that
self-doubts hit her like a ton of bricks falling on her
head. What had she just done? With the bravado that
had often gotten her into trouble in the past, she'd just
announced that she intended to defend Dominic Marcola against a murder charge. It would be her first murder case. In fact, it would be her first case of any kind.

What bothered her was that she wasn't sure she was
taking the case because she believed in Dominic and
wanted to help him, or because she wanted to prove
something to Tyler Sinclair.

Chaos had returned. That was Tyler's thought the
moment she whirled out of his office. He'd always

known she would come home eventually. What he hadn't expected was that she would come bearing a law degree.

He leaned back in the chair, the photocopy of her degree in hand. What a surprise. He'd assumed he would be able to buy her out, that Justice Inc. would be all his. He'd put blood, sweat and tears into the firm, always with Jamison's promise that someday it would belong to him. He hadn't counted on Samantha getting a degree and wanting to be a working partner.

Somehow he knew he shouldn't be surprised. Samantha had always managed to do the unexpected. That had always been part of her charm, and part of what had once driven him utterly crazy.

He didn't want her in the firm, didn't want her in his life in any way, shape or form. She muddled his senses, made the irrational appear rational, made him think of dreams he'd long ago cast aside. She was a threat to everything he'd worked so hard to achieve.

He cast the photocopy aside, leaned back in his chair and closed his eyes, a vision of her unfolding in his mind. Hair askew, with flashing brown eyes and her dress decorated with wrinkles and what had appeared to be a splash of catsup on the bodice, she'd been as beautiful as he remembered.

Unlike her younger sister, who seemed to go out of her way to follow every rule, abide by laws both common and otherwise, Samantha had never met a rule she wouldn't break. She could lie without batting an eyelash, and she had a gift for the gab that had gotten her out of more than one tense situation. He smiled wryly. She would make one hell of a lawyer.

She couldn't be serious about taking the Marcola

case. It would be career suicide. His eyes narrowed as he thought of her assessment that he only took easy cases and thus had earned a reputation as a winning lawyer. It wasn't true. He'd had his share of difficult clients, overwhelming damning evidence, and painful losses.

What bothered him about the Marcola case was that it had all the elements of a sleazy tabloid story. Already it had not only filled the local papers, but had been picked up by the nearby Kansas City papers, as well. It would be a media madhouse, and Tyler wanted no part in it. Besides, Justice Inc. had always steered clear of murder cases.

Unfortunately, if Samantha was serious about representing Dominic, and Dominic agreed to her representation, Tyler had a feeling he would be sucked into the whole mess. Yes, chaos had returned, and its name was Samantha.

Chapter 2

The Dark mansion sat atop a hill overlooking the small town of Wilford, Kansas, the way the manor of a feudal lord would dominate his kingdom.

For all intents and purposes, Jamison Dark had been king of Wilford. He'd owned half the land in town and had been a powerful friend to his supporters, a wicked foe to anyone who opposed him.

The porch light was lit, as if in warm welcome as she pulled up in the circular driveway. But Samantha knew the implied welcome was merely an illusion. The house had never contained any warmth or family affection. It had been cold and austere, a perfect reflection of her father.

She knocked on the front door, wondering if the dragon lady still ran the household with an iron fist. Sure enough, Virginia Wilcox opened the door, her dark eyes flaring slightly in surprise. "Samantha." She said the name as if it left a sour taste in her mouth.

"Hello, Virginia."

Samantha stepped around the rigid-backed, gray-haired woman. Familiar scents assailed her—the smell of lemon furniture polish mingled with woodsmoke from the fireplace in the den. Her father had always loved a fire and only on the hottest of nights did the fireplace remain dormant.

Although Virginia displayed no further emotion, Samantha felt both her surprise and her displeasure as she set down her battered suitcase. "Is my room available?" she asked.

"Of course. Mr. Tyler called a few minutes ago and had me prepare it."

Samantha nodded and picked up her suitcase, sighing in dismay as the burgeoning case snapped open and clothes spilled out. "I'll get it," she said, despite the fact that Virginia hadn't moved. "You can go back to whatever you were doing. I know the way to my room."

Virginia nodded and left the foyer, moving in silence like a disapproving wraith. Samantha watched her go, then bent down to grab a handful of the clothing. It took her only a minute to realize she would have to make two trips. There was no way to stuff her clothes back into the broken suitcase.

She took the wide, winding staircase two steps at a time, wondering which room Tyler called home. Probably the blue bedroom. She could see him in that room with its masculine furniture and the navy blue and silver wallpaper.

Before passing it by, she stopped and opened the door and peeked inside. Sure enough, the room smelled of his cologne and the closet was open, displaying suits neatly hung.

She closed the door and continued down the long hallway to her own bedroom. Thank goodness. At least for the time she was here, he would be at one end of the hall and her room was at the other.

It didn't surprise her that he lived here. She'd been fourteen when her father had first introduced her to his protégé. It had been obvious from that moment that Tyler would receive from her father all the love, respect and friendship she herself had craved. It was then that she had begun to hate Tyler Sinclair.

Shoving these thoughts aside, she pushed open the door to her bedroom. It was just as she'd left it six years ago. A feminine white bed with a blush-colored ruffled bedspread, the one she'd picked out for herself when she was twelve years old.

She threw the armful of clothes on the bed and walked around the room, touching old mementos and keepsakes as memories sailed through her mind. Here was the music box given to her by Samuel Edwards, a boy her father had considered unsuitable for a Dark daughter. There was the stuffed animal, won for her at a carnival that had come through town when she was sixteen.

Her fingers found her initials, carved into the side of the dresser. A tinge of shame coursed through her as she realized the destructiveness, remembered the childish glee she'd felt when she placed them here—as if by marring the furniture she could hurt her father.

She'd spent a lot of time in this room, usually sent here for some infraction of her father's rigid rules. As she'd grown older, she'd found other places to hide out from her father's condemnation, places far less appropriate.

She'd made a lot of bad choices in the impetuousness

of youth, and she was sorry her father wouldn't be here
to see the woman she'd finally become.

"Would you like something to eat?"

Samantha gasped and whirled around to see Virginia
standing in her doorway. The woman moved like a jun-
gle animal, stealthily and without a sound. "No. No,
thank you."

"Then I'll be leaving for the night."

"Before you go, do you happen to know my sister's
phone number?" Samantha asked.

Virginia's features softened. "Of course. She calls
nearly every day."

"Hang on, let me get a piece of paper and a pencil."
Samantha grabbed her purse and dug around in the bottom to find the required items. Of course Melissa called
every day. She'd always been the "good daughter."
"Okay," Samantha said, pencil in hand.

Virginia reeled off the number in her dry, unfriendly
tone.

"Thanks. I'll see you in the morning."

With a curt nod of her head, Virginia stole away. A
few minutes later Samantha heard the distant roar of a
car engine and knew Virginia had gone for the night.

She stared down at the number in her hand, wondering what Melissa was doing at this moment. The two
had never been particularly close, but there had been
odd moments in the past six years when Samantha had
desperately missed her sister.

Without giving herself a chance for second thoughts,
Samantha sat on the edge of the bed and picked up the
receiver of the phone on the nightstand. She punched
in the seven numbers and waited.

It was answered on the second ring as Melissa's familiar voice filled the line.

"Melissa, it's Samantha," she announced.

A stunned silence followed. Then, "I wondered if we'd hear from you. Where are you?"

"In Wilford. At the house. I'm sorry I missed the funeral."

"Everyone in town attended. You'd have thought a celebrity passed away." Melissa's voice sounded stilted, strained. "How long are you in town for?"

"I intend to stay." Samantha wished she could reach back through the years, embrace the little girl who had once followed her like a shadow. But she knew that little girl was gone, shoved aside by a big sister who'd had too much anger in her to cope with a sibling. "I'd like to see you. Maybe we could have lunch tomorrow?"

Again there was a long pause, as if Melissa wasn't sure she wanted to meet Samantha for lunch. "Okay. I'd like that."

Samantha eased her grip on the receiver in relief. "Great. Where shall we meet?"

"How about the club?"

Samantha hesitated for a moment. She'd always hated the country club, but she suddenly realized she would agree to meet her sister in hell if that was what she wanted. "Sounds fine. I'll see you there about noon," she agreed.

They said goodbye and Samantha hung up the receiver, her head filled with thoughts of her sister. Tyler had said her sister was separated. Why wasn't Melissa living here? Where was she living? So many questions. Maybe...just maybe it wasn't too late for the two of them to become friends.

Without the interference of their father, maybe they

could finally find the sisterly love that had somehow been misplaced through the years.

She'd never much minded being alone, but now she realized there was a difference between being alone and being lonely. For the last several years of her life, she'd been lonely.

In her distant memory echoed the laughter of two little girls and their mother. When their mother died, the laughter had gone with her and the two little girls had drifted apart.

"It's not too late," Samantha whispered to herself softly. It wasn't too late to recapture that closeness she'd once felt with Melissa. It would take time and patience; and while Samantha had always been short of patience, she had plenty of time.

With memories of her mother still drifting through her head, Samantha left her bedroom and went down the hall to the room that had once belonged to her mother. She opened the door and stepped into the darkness.

For a moment she imagined she smelled her mother's perfume, a sweet blend of florals and spices. She breathed deeply, wishing she could forever capture the essence of her mother. When she opened her eyes, she realized her imagination had gotten the best of her and what she really smelled was the stuffy mustiness of a room that had been closed up for too long.

She flipped on the light and looked around. After all this time, everything remained exactly as it had been when her mother was alive. The dainty vanity top still displayed her perfume bottles and beauty creams as if she'd merely stepped out for an evening's entertainment and would return at any moment. Despite the slight musty scent, the room appeared clean. Virginia must come in and dust occasionally, Samantha thought.

Samantha had never understood her father, who had never shed a tear nor displayed any kind of grief over his wife's death, and yet he had refused to allow anyone to change this particular room. It was the kind of senseless dichotomy he'd often displayed. Even she and her sister had been forbidden to come in here for as long as Samantha could remember.

With a curious sense of dread, she slowly walked toward the gold brocade curtains drawn tightly closed over the glass French doors that led onto the balcony.

Hands trembling slightly, she drew the curtains back and opened the doors. Cool night air caressed her as she stepped out onto the balcony. Directly ahead of her was a gaping hole in the railing, a new board nailed across the opening for some measure of safety.

After her mother had fallen to her death so many years ago, Samantha could remember Virginia pleading with Jamison to tear down the balcony and board up the French doors. But it had never been done. The balcony had remained, weathering year after year. How ironic that her father had died falling the same way his wife had.

Again she had the feeling that something was amiss. She could never recall a time when her father had entered this room. And he would never, ever have set foot onto this balcony. Despite Jamison's powerful personality, his overwhelming strength of character, he'd had an innate fear of heights.

Samantha approached the railing cautiously and peered down at the concrete terrace below. What had her father been doing out here? What could possibly have forced him to ignore his deep-seated fear and walk out on the balcony?

"You shouldn't be out here."

A sharp scream of surprise escaped her at the deep voice.

She whirled around to see Tyler standing in the doorway. "What are you trying to do, give me a heart attack?" she snapped. She pushed past him to get back into the house, her legs shaky from the fright he'd given her.

"I believe these are yours." He held out a handful of her lingerie. A wispy lavender bra and panties escaped his grasp and fell to the floor. "They were in the foyer."

A hot blush washed over her as she hurriedly picked up the errant underwear and grabbed the rest from his hand. "My suitcase broke," she explained. Then, quickly changing the subject, she said, "I want to see my father's autopsy report."

He blinked. She'd obviously caught him by surprise. "You'll have to get it from the medical examiner. I don't have a copy." He narrowed his eyes. "What hornet's nest are you stirring up, Samantha?"

"I don't intend to stir up anything," she replied. He followed her out of her mother's room and down the hallway. "I just want to know whatever details there are about my father's death." She paused in her doorway and tossed the handful of underwear at her bed, then headed down the stairs. "Why don't you have a drink with me and fill me in on what's been happening since I left?"

Tyler followed her downstairs with a slight feeling of trepidation. She'd been home less than an hour and upheaval had been evident the moment he'd stepped into the foyer and spied the silk underthings all over the floor.

They'd felt obscenely smooth and cool in his grasp, and he'd immediately been able to envision her slender, shapely form in the pale purple panties and whisper of a bra.

The fire Virginia had started for them in the den snapped and crackled pleasantly. As she walked to the bar, Tyler sat down on the sofa, hoping she wouldn't drink enough to repeat the seduction she'd tried on him so many years ago. He was tired and felt an edge of crankiness; he certainly didn't want an unpleasant scene.

"Name your poison," she said from behind the marble-topped wet bar.

"Brandy."

She nodded and splashed a couple of inches of the amber liquor into the bottom of a snifter. She then poured a liberal amount of club soda into a glass and added a slice of lime.

"Don't look so surprised," she said dryly as she handed him the snifter. "The last time I drank was the night you rescued me from the James bar. I realized that night that alcohol made me stupid."

He didn't remember her stupid. He remembered her sexy as hell, a wanton flame of heat that had nearly made him throw away everything he'd worked for, including his own self-respect. "So, you've completed law school and stopped drinking. Commendable behavior."

"Behavior proper for a Dark," she replied with a touch of sarcasm and sat down next to him.

He smiled and swirled the brandy in the bottom of

his glass. "There's something to be said for proper behavior."

"Not when it sucks the very life out of you." She cast him a sideways glance beneath her thick lashes. "Besides, sometimes improper behavior is far more fun."

He kept his smile, although his blood warmed enticingly. "There's nothing wrong with playing by the rules."

Her brown eyes skimmed him curiously, as if he were an odd, new species. "Tell me something, Tyler. Were you always a rigid stick-in-the-mud, or did my father turn you into one?"

He laughed, as always finding her an odd mix of charming candor and irritating brashness. "Tell me something, Samantha. Are you ever going to grow out of being a mouthy, rebellious brat?"

For a moment they battled with their eyes, each refusing to look away. It was finally she who averted her gaze and laughed softly. "Stalemate."

He nodded and sipped his brandy, watching as she stood and paced the floor in front of the fire. At twenty-nine, she'd blossomed into the beauty that he'd anticipated years ago. The mouth that had always seemed a trifle too wide now appeared to fit perfectly in her face. Her eyes held shadows that gave her a mysterious appeal.

Yes, she had always been a beauty, and that hadn't changed. Nor had he changed his mind about what he wanted in a woman—attributes that Samantha Dark would never possess.

Still, he was aware that Samantha represented a forbidden danger to him. If he were a different kind of man, he wouldn't mind a single night of passion shared with her, but any more than that would ruin all the dreams, all the plans he'd made for himself.

Despite the physical attraction he'd always felt for her, he didn't intend for her to mess up his personal life, nor did he intend to see her ruin his professional life by gambling with Dominic Marcola's life.

"Samantha, you can't take the Marcola case."

She stopped pacing, her back stiffening as her eyes flared wide. Immediately he regretted his words. He knew better than to use the word *can't* with Samantha. It was like waving a red flag in front of a bull. "Yes, I can. If Dominic agrees to let me represent him, then that's exactly what I intend to do."

"You don't even know the details of the case," he objected.

"I'll learn them."

"It's going to be a high-profile case."

She shrugged and gave him an irreverent grin. "I think my picture will look fine in the papers."

He took a sip of his brandy, wishing it were something even stronger. "You'll be in over your head," he finally managed softly.

"It won't be the first time." She sank down next to him on the sofa. "If you don't want me to take the case, then you do it."

He shook his head. "I won't. I can't. I never handle cases like this."

"But you try criminal cases," she protested.

"Not murder cases. Samantha, I'm not going to represent Dominic Marcola and that's that." There was no way he would tell her the real reason he couldn't. He'd buried that baggage a long time ago and never intended to expose it to anyone.

"You're not giving me any valid reasons," she pressed.

"I don't owe you any explanations for the decisions I make," he returned.

"Then I'll represent him," she declared. He could see her frustration in her body language. "As a fifty-percent partner in this firm, I'll have all the firm's resources at my fingertips, just as you do."

"And what happens if he really is guilty?"

She flinched, as if the thought had never entered her mind. "Then I'll see what the mitigating circumstances are and see that he gets the best deal possible."

Before he realized it, she was sitting so close to him he could smell the subtle scent of her perfume, see the tiny mole that rode just to the left of her lower lip.

"Don't you see?" she pleaded. "Defending people who can't defend themselves is what I went to law school for."

This was a side of Samantha he'd never seen before. Earnest, with eyes shining almost feverishly. Why was this case so important to her? What was Dominic Marcola to her?

"This particular case is too big to cut your teeth on," he said. "Dominic is facing the death penalty. He should have the best, not a greenhorn lawyer who doesn't know her way around a courtroom."

She frowned. "The best won't take the case. Besides, I have an advantage over another lawyer."

"And what's that?"

"Unlike all the other lawyers I've ever known, I still have a heart, and my heart says Dominic is innocent."

Tyler finished his brandy and carried his glass back to the bar. He turned to face her once again. "This is a business that will steal any heart you have, Samantha.

It's not a career you dabble in because you're bored or trying to prove something.''

Her eyes sparked as she stood, her back stiffening defensively. He'd made her angry again. "I'm not playing at this. I'm not some poor little rich girl dabbling in the law, and I resent that implication." She tossed her head and eyed him loftily. "What are you really afraid of, Tyler? That I'll be good? Maybe better than you? Maybe, just maybe you're afraid I'll be so good I'll usurp your position as the best lawyer in Kansas."

He walked over to where she stood vibrating with energy. She held her ground, despite the fact that he'd moved close enough to invade her personal space. "Is that what this is about, Samantha? You aren't so much interested in defending Dominic as you want to best me?"

He reached a hand up and stroked the side of her face. She allowed the caress, her eyes narrowed but unflinching. He marveled at the smoothness of her skin, the heat that spoke of such life, such passion. "You're playing in a game that's way over your head. The one with no heart almost always wins."

She stepped back from him, her face flushed with color. "This all might be moot. Dominic may not want me to represent him."

He dropped his hand and laughed wryly. "Samantha, I doubt our good law-enforcement officer has a chance against your wiles. If you want to be his counsel, he'll agree. You could talk the devil into buying fire sticks." And the reputation of Justice Inc. will rest in your hands, he grimly and silently added.

"We'll know for sure tomorrow. I intend to talk to Dominic first thing in the morning." She looked at her watch. "And on that note, I think I'll head off to bed.

It's been a long day and tomorrow promises to be even longer.''

Yes, tomorrow promised to be even longer, Tyler agreed as he watched her climb the stairs. He poured himself a second glass of brandy and sat down in front of the fire. As he stared into the hypnotic flames, he thought of Jamison Jackson Dark.

The old man would spin in his grave if he knew Samantha's intentions. Justice Inc. had always been a firm that catered to the white-collar crimes of the well-to-do, and kept away from publicity-drenched cases where careers were made famous by the press.

Of course, Jamison wouldn't have been surprised by his eldest daughter's plans. Samantha had spent most of her teenage and early adult years flirting with trouble, making poor choices, playing the role of bad girl in what Tyler had suspected was an effort to gain her father's attention.

Jamison had been a brilliant man…but difficult. He'd inspired fear, respect, but rarely love. Still, he'd given Tyler a chance to become something, someone. In Tyler he'd seen something worth salvaging, and for that, Tyler would always be grateful—grateful enough not to allow Samantha to ruin everything her father and he had worked for over the years….

Samantha didn't like Tyler, had never liked him. He was a prude, a miniature clone of her father, filled with the same self-righteousness and pompous arrogance.

Yet, there was something about Tyler that evoked a strong passion in her. Perhaps it was his enigmatic mystique. She knew nothing about his past, nothing about where he'd come from. He'd simply appeared in their lives one day and never left.

He'd commanded their father's respect, stolen any love he might have had for his daughters. He'd become the son their father had always wanted, and for that Samantha hated him.

She'd often heard the two of them in the den, their deep masculine laughter ringing out as they shared pieces of their day. It was a ritual of male bonding that had excluded and enraged Samantha.

She hung up the last of her clothes and walked over to her window. Drawing aside the curtain, she peered outside. From this vantage point she could see the balcony that jutted out from her mother's bedroom.

Again, questions flitted through her head. Why had her father walked out there? In all her years of living at home, she'd never once seen her father in her mother's room, let alone out on that deadly balcony. What had possessed him to walk out there and lean against a rotting railing?

Suicide? Somehow she couldn't imagine her father taking his own life, no matter what the circumstances. So what were the alternatives? An accident that didn't make sense?

Or murder?

A chill danced up her arms at that thought. Was it possible he hadn't accidentally fallen, but instead had been pushed?

She dropped the curtain back in place and moved away from the window. Always when a murder was committed, the number-one question was who might gain from such a murder.

Certainly she and her sister had gained from their father's death, but the idea that Melissa had anything to do with his death was absurd.

Samantha sank down on the bed. There was only one

other person who had a lot to gain from Jamison Jackson Dark's death. Tyler. She frowned and rubbed her forehead; the headache she'd fought off earlier now blossomed with nauseating force.

The thought of Tyler committing murder was equally as ridiculous as the thought of Melissa having anything to do with such a horrible crime. Impossible. No matter how much Samantha didn't like Tyler, she knew he wasn't anything close to a killer.

She touched her face, remembering the feel of his hand on her there. For just a moment, her heart had leaped at his touch. She shook her head, dispelling this particular phenomenon.

She was tired, and fanciful thoughts always came to her more easily then. The idea that her heart had reacted to the touch of Tyler's hand was definitely fanciful. Tyler meant less than nothing to her. At the moment he was merely an unwanted partner in a business.

She needed to keep focused on the problems at hand—and she had plenty. She wanted to further explore the circumstances of her father's death. She needed to gear herself up for a legal battle to save Dominic, and more than anything, she wanted to find a way to force Tyler Sinclair out of the law firm—and out of her life.

Chapter 3

Samantha woke earlier than usual, after a restless night. She showered and dressed in one of her few two-piece suits, knowing she needed to look like a professional for her jailhouse visit with Dominic.

A few minutes later she eyed herself in the bathroom mirror as her fingers nimbly worked to capture her wild hair into a twist at the nape of her neck.

Hair finally as neat as the curly mass could get, she stepped away from the mirror and eyed herself critically. The navy skirt was shorter than she'd remembered, and her lipstick was a trifle too bright. She wiped her mouth with a tissue, tugged at her skirt, then left the bathroom and went downstairs in search of a cup of coffee.

The scent of fresh brew struck her as she walked into the large, formal dining room. On the antique wooden buffet, a serving tray with a coffee carafe sat ready. She made a beeline toward it, poured herself a cup and sat down at the ornate, highly polished table.

The morning newspaper rested on top of the table, but she didn't pick it up. She didn't want to read anything about the Marcola case, preferring to get her first impression of the case from her potential client. Many accused had been judged and tried by the media, and she wasn't about to get caught up in believing anything other than the true facts of the case.

Sipping her coffee, she tried to keep her focus on her upcoming meeting with Dominic. She didn't want her mind cluttered with all of her other troubling thoughts.

She smelled the subtle, spicy cologne and knew Tyler approached before she saw him. She turned her head in the direction of the doorway as his scent preceded him into the room.

He stopped in the doorway, as if surprised to see her. "Good morning," he said and headed for the coffee carafe. "I remember the days when you didn't make an appearance until noon," he observed as he carried his cup to the table and sat across from her.

"Those were the days when I didn't think I had a reason to get up. Now I do." She grinned at his frown. "Did you think maybe I'd change my mind about the Marcola case overnight?"

"I'd hoped sleep might bring sanity," he said wryly.

"Not a chance." She sipped her coffee, studying him as he flipped open the paper and scanned the front page.

Physically, he was the type of man that Samantha had always found attractive. All darkness and shadows, a hint of secrets in his eyes. The aura of suppressed emotions flirting dangerously with exposure. He looked like a bad boy in a three-piece suit. And Samantha had always had a thing for bad boys.

Yes, Tyler had the look of a bad boy, but he had the personality of a proper, staid old man, complete with an expression of disapproving disdain that had the capacity to enrage her.

She got up and poured herself another cup of coffee, then checked her watch. Another fifteen minutes or so and she would leave to meet Dominic. She hoped he agreed to take her on as counsel. She desperately wanted his case, needed this case to prove to everyone, including herself, that she could do something good, something worthwhile.

She didn't care what Tyler said. She felt as if fate had stepped in and handed her this opportunity to do something positive. And for once in her life, she intended not to blow it.

"I'd like to go with you to meet Dominic," Tyler said as he refolded the paper.

She looked at him in surprise. "Why? I thought you didn't want anything to do with the case."

"I don't," he admitted. "But if you insist on going through with representing him, then as the only other partner in the firm, I should know exactly what's going on."

Samantha shrugged. "Suit yourself."

"Besides," he continued, "I've worked too hard gaining a reputation of legal competence. I don't want you making stupid mistakes that might result in a mistrial or anything that will reflect poorly on the firm."

Samantha's back stiffened at his words. He was so pompous. "My stupid mistakes are behind me, and I wouldn't take this case unless I felt that I was more than competent."

He smiled coolly. "The stakes are mighty high if you're wrong."

"Yeah, but if I'm right, I might topple you off your throne of greatness," she retorted.

He laughed, and the deep, unexpected melodic sound of it sent a shiver up Samantha's spine. He sobered then, a telling, disapproving wrinkle creasing his forehead. "Just remember, your goal is to defend Dominic, not seize my throne."

"I'm well aware of the ultimate goal," she replied. She finished her coffee and stood. "I'll see you at the jail, partner."

Moments later as she drove to the jailhouse located in the center of the small town of Wilford, she tried to decide how Tyler Sinclair managed to get under her skin so easily. It had always been that way. For as long as she could remember he'd been able to stir her up seemingly without much effort on his part.

It didn't help that he'd been witness to everything she'd ever done in the name of youthful rebellion. He'd been there the night her father had caught her climbing the trellis to her bedroom after curfew. He'd been present when she'd returned—kicked out and disgraced— from college.

And of course, he'd been the one to pull her out of that seedy bar, where she'd bellied up and drunk too much, then found herself in a threatening situation. Her face burned as she remembered her attempted seduction of him as he'd driven her home.

Grief tore through her as she thought of her father and the fact that he would never know she'd finally grown up, that her foolish, self-destructive behavior was behind her. He would never know how she'd struggled on her own to get through college and law school, working menial jobs to support herself in an effort to make him proud.

She knew deep in her heart that her need to take on Dominic's case was an attempt to prove to herself and her late father, once and for all, that she was smart, and good, and worthy of the Dark name.

She emptied her mind of all thoughts as she pulled into the parking area behind the Wilford Police Department. Time to focus on the task at hand and put aside any personal emotional baggage she might carry from her past.

The Wilford Police Department was housed in a two-story building erected in 1927. The structure showed its age in the crumbling bricks and weathered window frames, and in the musty, ancient scent that greeted Samantha when she walked in the front door.

She knew the ground floor handled actual police business and the second floor housed the county prosecutor's office. She wondered vaguely who the prosecutor was now and if she would go head-to-head with him or one of the underlings. She had a feeling the head honcho himself would be prosecuting this particular high-profile case.

In the basement of the building were the county jail cells. She'd just started down the stairway when Tyler caught up with her.

"Sort of like entering the dungeon of the damned, don't you think?" she said.

"Wilford could definitely use an updated jail," he agreed. "Unfortunately, the taxpayers keep voting no to funding for such a project."

When they reached the bottom of the stairs, a uniformed guard stopped them and asked for identification and the purpose of their visit. He then led them to a small room used for meetings between inmates and counsel.

The room contained nothing more than a folding table and several chairs. Samantha set her briefcase on the table and sat down. Tyler leaned against the wall, his arms crossed in front of him.

"Aren't you going to sit down?" she asked him.

He shook his head. "I don't want Dominic to think in any way I'm going to be a part of his defense."

"Then you shouldn't have come."

He smiled thinly. "I'm protecting what's mine."

"*Half* yours," she reminded him.

At that moment the door opened and Dominic was led inside by two guards, shackles and all. His dark eyes flared in surprise as he looked first at Samantha, then at Tyler. He didn't say a word until the guards had unchained him and left the room.

Samantha tried to hide her dismay at his appearance. When she'd last seen him, he'd been so strong, so vital looking. Now his face reflected a jailhouse pallor, and he appeared to have lost weight.

"When did you get back into town?" he asked Samantha.

"Yesterday." She gestured to the chair across from her.

"Thank God," he breathed as he sank down at the table, his gaze lingering on Tyler. "Dad said he was trying to get Mr. Sinclair to take my case, but I didn't think there was a chance in hell he'd be interested."

"Mr. Sinclair isn't here to take your case. He's merely here as an interested representative of Justice Inc.," Samantha explained.

Dominic frowned at her words. "Then what exactly are you both doing here?"

"I'm here to offer you my representation," Samantha explained. "Pro bono."

Tyler swallowed his gasp of surprise. He'd had no idea she intended to represent Dominic at the expense of the firm.

Dominic stared at her for a long moment. "You're a lawyer?"

"I'm a damn good lawyer," she replied. She carefully kept her gaze averted from Tyler, afraid she would see doubt or amusement in his eyes. "I'd like to be your lawyer."

Dominic's eyes played over her, searching her features as if seeking answers of some kind. He finally nodded. "All right. I guess you can't be any worse than if I randomly picked a name out of the phone book."

Samantha tried to smile at that, then withdrew a pad and pen from her briefcase. "Now, tell me exactly what happened the night of Abigail Monroe's murder." She frowned, slightly distracted by Tyler's sexy scent as he joined them at the table.

She wished he hadn't come. Something about him made her self-conscious, ill at ease. If he corrected her about anything in front of Dominic, she had a feeling she would be joining Dominic in a cell. She would kill Tyler if he corrected her, kill him for undermining not only her confidence in herself, but Dominic's confidence in her, as well. With effort, she forced her attention away from her handsome partner and onto her new client.

It took Dominic only minutes to explain that before Abigail's marriage to the wealthy older banker, Morgan Monroe, she and Dominic had had a relationship. Abigail had married Monroe on a whim, preferring the lifestyle the wealthy banker could provide to the life Dominic could offer her. However, she'd made it clear she hoped the relationship with Dominic would continue.

Dominic had declined, having no interest in an adulterous liaison with no future.

According to Dominic, he'd seen very little of Abigail during the two months of her marriage; then on the evening of the murder, she'd called him, sounding jubilant. She'd begged him to come over, insisting she needed to talk to him. Reluctantly he'd agreed.

As Dominic spoke, Samantha took copious notes, carefully keeping her expression blank.

When he got to Abigail's, she had greeted him with excitement. "She was manic," Dominic explained. "She poured champagne and said we were celebrating, but refused to tell me anything more until we'd each had several glasses of the bubbly."

Dominic raked a hand through his thick, dark hair, his features taut with tension. "I've never had champagne hit me like that. After two glasses I got a little woozy."

"Go on," Samantha urged, seeing in his eyes how difficult this was for him. Although Tyler didn't say a word, he leaned forward, as if knowing that whatever Dominic had to relate next would be the crux of the crime.

"She finally told me the marriage had been a mistake, but she'd come up with something that would allow her to leave Monroe with a very healthy divorce settlement. We had more champagne, then this is where things get fuzzy."

Samantha noticed that Dominic's hands shook and he clasped them together on top of the table to still their trembling. He closed his eyes and when he finally looked at her again, dark torture radiated from him. "She wanted to make love. She started to undress, but I stopped her. We fought. She stomped into the bedroom and I followed her. She started to undress again and we struggled. We fell onto the bed, and that's all I remember.''

He expelled a deep breath, then continued. "When I came to, I was on the bed. Abigail was next to me, naked...and dead, strangled with a scarf. Before I had time to figure out exactly what had happened, two officers broke into the room and placed me under arrest for her murder.''

Samantha frowned. "How did the officers get there? What made them show up at that time?''

Dominic shrugged. "I heard that somebody made a phone call, said that Abigail was screaming and it sounded like she was in danger.''

Samantha frowned again and made several notes to herself on the legal pad. They spoke for a few more minutes, Samantha asking questions, then listening intently to his replies and jotting down notes.

"I didn't kill her, Samantha. Somebody is setting me up to take this fall. I swear, I didn't do it. I couldn't have. I loved her.''

"I know, and I'm going to work as hard as I can to prove that to a jury.'' Samantha covered his hands with one of hers. "We're going to get you out of this mess,'' she said firmly.

Dominic shook his head. "You're a lot more optimistic than I am. I'm a cop. I know how bad the evidence looks against me.''

"Just do me a favor—don't talk to anyone about any of the circumstances of this case,'' Samantha advised. She stood and threw her pen and pad into her briefcase, then snapped it closed. "The only person you talk to is me. I'll be back to see you in a day or two and we'll talk more, outline our defense strategy.''

Samantha walked over to the heavy steel door and motioned to the guard outside that they were finished. Dominic stood as guards came in to take him back to his cell. As Samantha watched Dominic being led away, she wondered if she'd bitten off more than she could chew. Again.

Despite his reservations, Tyler had to admit he was impressed by Samantha's skill. She'd asked the questions a good defense lawyer would ask, and she hadn't appeared rattled by the incriminating answers.

As they walked back up the stairs, Tyler pondered why her very competence somehow irritated him. Was it because she displayed so naturally the qualities he'd had to work long and hard to possess?

Or was it because her skirt had been too damned short, exposing a sinful length of shapely leg? There should be a law against legs like hers.

As he followed behind her, he noted the sexy sway of her hips beneath the short skirt. There should be a law against the way she walked, as well.

"Do you have to go right to the office or do you have a few minutes for a cup of coffee?" she asked as they reached the door leading outside. "I've got a few things to go over with you."

He didn't want to meet her for coffee, was sorry he'd come here in the first place. "It will have to be a quick cup," he surprised himself by saying.

She nodded. "Is that little café still on the corner of Oak and Main?"

"Yes, the Corner Café."

"I'll meet you there." She whirled on her heels.

As she walked toward her car, the autumn breeze

flirted with the hem of her skirt, causing it to lift to a higher level of danger. Tyler's ire rose accordingly.

I should have just gone straight to the office this morning, he told himself as he got into his car and headed for the nearby café. Only one day back in town and already Samantha was turning his world upside down.

After her father's death he'd been shocked when he learned the contents of Jamison's will—that Jamison had split the firm between Tyler and his eldest, rebellious daughter. Tyler had felt betrayed by the man he'd considered his surrogate father, the man who had made it clear for years that one day Justice Inc. would belong to Tyler.

In the last two years of his life, Jamison had done little of the actual work at the firm. He'd depended on Tyler to carry the workload while he enjoyed a semi-retirement of sorts. Tyler hadn't minded. He'd considered he was investing in his future—a future he now shared with Samantha.

He pulled into a parking space in front of the Corner Café. Damn Jamison for splitting the firm. And damn the man for binding Tyler to his daughter.

Tyler had one single ray of hope. If Samantha proved true to her past, she would either do something outrageous and run away again, or she would tire of the work and emotional drain of the job and quit.

The moment he walked into the café, despite the crowded interior, he spied her immediately. It was as if he had a built-in homing device where she was concerned. Again his irritation rose irrationally.

He worked his way through the crowd, mostly senior citizens who received free coffee every Tuesday morning at the café. Somehow, either through luck or sweet talk, Samantha had managed to get one of the coveted high-backed booths near the fire exit. There were only three such booths, the high backs providing a sort of privacy from the rest of the patrons.

"I ordered coffee for us both," she said as he slid in across from her. "Cream for you, right?"

"Right," he replied, surprised that she would remember such a little thing as how he drank his coffee. "So, what did you want to talk to me about?"

"What investigative company do we use?" she asked.

Tyler smiled. Obviously she expected this to be easy. "We don't have an investigative company we use."

A tiny wrinkle marred her forehead as she frowned. "I don't understand. Surely you use somebody to do legwork—a private investigator of some sort?"

"Most of the cases we handle don't require a lot of legwork, and what little is required, I do myself." He smiled at her deepening frown. "I warned you, Samantha, that we usually don't take cases like Dominic's. For the most part, our load is civil cases that don't demand a lot of investigation."

The conversation ceased momentarily as the waitress appeared to serve their coffee. "Can I get you anything else?" she asked brightly and they both shook their heads.

"But I know Father used somebody several years ago. I remember meeting him in the office one afternoon," Samantha continued, the moment the waitress had departed.

"You probably met Wylie Brooks. A burly bald man?"

"Yes, that's him."

"Wylie spends most of his days fishing. He retired

about six months ago.'' Tyler leaned forward. ''Samantha, you aren't going to find anyone from around here
to help you with this. Morgan Monroe is not only respected in this town, he's powerful. Morgan Invest-
ments services half the mortgages in Wilford.''

''Well, he doesn't service mine. Everything Father
owned was paid off free and clear, and one of the first
things I want to know is exactly what kind of alibi Mr.
Morgan Monroe has for the night of the murder. You
know the husband is often the most likely suspect.''

''Airtight,'' Tyler replied. ''At the time of the murder, Morgan was seventy miles away giving a speech
at an investment-opportunity banquet. He's got a hundred witnesses to his presence there.''

Tyler leaned against the back of the booth. He could
almost feel sorry for her, with the helpless frustration
that created the fetching wrinkle in the center of her
brow. But he had warned her.

''I don't understand. When you represented that
young woman on the stalking case several months ago,
you didn't use an investigator?'' she asked.

Surprise whipped through him. He grinned lazily.
''You managed to follow my career from out of town?''

''Don't flatter yourself,'' she snapped, her cheeks
flushing a becoming pink. ''I told you before, I had a
subscription to the Wilford paper. I just happen to have
read an article about that particular case.'' She eyed him
critically. ''What's the difference between it and Dominic's?''

Tyler took a sip of his coffee, then grinned at her
once again. ''Samantha, there's a big difference between a murder case and a stalking one.''

''Yeah, Dominic could get the electric chair, while

the stalker was only looking at a couple of years in prison.'' She tilted her head, her gaze still curious.

"The stalking case didn't end up with anyone dead. It was fairly cut-and-dried, of little interest to anyone other than the people involved.''

"But it was a criminal case,'' Samantha pressed. "Father never did criminal cases. How did you get him to let Justice Inc. get involved?''

Tyler hesitated. "To tell the truth, I didn't tell him I'd taken it on until it was too late for me to pull out.''

Samantha's eyes flickered with surprised amusement. "What? The perfect boy rebels in secret against his beloved mentor?'' One of her pale eyebrows danced upward mockingly. "I must say, I'm shocked. I didn't know you had it in you.''

Her tone irritated him. She was so certain he was nothing but a shadow of Jamison, so certain he was nothing but a bore, an uptight prig. He leaned forward and encircled her wrist with his fingers. He felt the rapid beating of her pulse beneath his index finger.

"You might be surprised at what rebellious, unseemly fantasies occasionally rush through my head,'' he said softly. Immediately he felt an increase in her pulse. The knowledge that his words had somehow stimulated her, aroused a dangerous fever.

He released her wrist and drew a steadying breath. "However, I pick and choose my rebellions very carefully, and I know fantasies are best left as unfulfilled illusions.'' Tyler's blood thickened, heated with the sexy secretiveness of her smile.

"Now that's where you're wrong, Tyler,'' she replied, her voice husky and low. "Some fantasies make wonderful reality. You just have to know which ones to reach out for and which ones to leave alone.''

"Are you sure you know the difference?" he asked, vaguely wondering how in the hell he'd lost control of the conversation.

She shrugged, the little smile still playing at the corners of her lips. "My judgment wasn't very good when I was younger, but I've learned a little discernment in the last couple of years." She leaned forward and he caught a whiff of her perfume. The scent reminded him of primal forests and clean rain—an earthy scent that stirred something primitive in him.

Tyler drained the last of his coffee and stood. "I've got to get to the office," he said.

Samantha stood as well. "Yes, and I need to get over to the courthouse and let the appropriate people know I'm Tony's counsel of record."

They each threw a dollar on the table, then left the café together. Once out on the sidewalk, Samantha placed a hand on his arm, her expression sober. "Don't worry, Tyler. I don't intend to mess up the reputation of Justice Inc. I intend to enhance it by proving Dominic is innocent."

"And how do you expect to do that?" he asked, amused at her confidence, her neophyte bravado.

"I'm going to find the real killer," she declared.

Before Tyler could react to her words, before he could tell her how dangerous such intentions could prove to be, she whipped around and walked toward her car.

Her short skirt swayed and bounced with each step, reminding Tyler of all the fantasies he'd ever entertained about her.

When she reached her car, she turned back to him, a grin still curving her lips. "Maybe later we can compare fantasies," she said, her voice carrying easily on the light autumn breeze. "I'd be more than happy to tell you which of yours are worth pursuing." She wiggled her fingers in a wave goodbye, then got into her car and pulled away from the café.

Tyler watched her go, his hands clenched at his sides. Drawing a deep breath, he forced himself to relax and headed for his own car. He wondered what she would say or do if he took her up on her offer, told her about the fantasies he'd once entertained about her? He had a feeling she wouldn't be amused to discover herself the central focus of his repressed sexual drive.

There had been a time when Samantha had occupied a space in his dreams—erotic dreams that had left him feeling frustrated and angry. At the time, he hadn't followed through on the fantasies because he'd respected Jamison too much, owed the man his very life and wouldn't repay that debt by sleeping with his wayward daughter.

Although Jamison was gone now, Tyler didn't want to become entangled in Samantha's life. Her life—her choices in life—represented the very sort of chaos Tyler had left behind.

Samantha had the ability to inspire passionate responses from those around her. She functioned out of emotion, thrived on anarchy.

Tyler had once been very much like Samantha, carrying around a burden of self-destructive anger. It had taken him years to put his past behind him, to learn to control the emotions that for too long had controlled him.

Tyler knew all too well the danger of passions exploding unchecked. He couldn't allow Samantha to take him back to that time of madness and murder. Those distant memories were what made it impossible for him to represent Dominic. And those same memories were what made any personal relationship with Samantha equally impossible.

Chapter 4

The Wilford Country Club was the town uppercrust's attempt to provide an exclusive playground for themselves. Surrounded by the golf course, the white, two-story building was a sprawling facility that offered an expensive restaurant on the first floor and gym facilities on the second. The yearly fee to maintain membership in the club was enough to feed a family of four for at least two years.

Samantha had never felt comfortable here, but her father had loved this place. He'd spent what free time he had in the dark, smoky bar adjoining the restaurant, where the ranking males gathered to discuss town politics and world affairs.

Although it shouldn't be so, nerves jangled inside Samantha at the prospect of lunching with her sister. The realization that seeing Melissa made her nervous, brought with it a tinge of sadness. It shouldn't be this way, she thought as she used the rearview mirror to fix

wayward tendrils that had escaped the confines of the
twist at the nape of her neck.

It saddened her that she and Melissa had gone such
separate ways, fallen so completely out of each other's
lives. Melissa was all the family Samantha had left, and
as Samantha got out of her car, she hoped it wasn't too
late to pick up the pieces and glue back some semblance
of a sisterly relationship.

There were few diners in the restaurant at this hour
of the day. A tableful of women sat in one corner, enjoying a round of drinks before ordering their lunch.

A good stiff drink would taste good, Samantha
thought, but instantly dismissed the idea. She'd learned
over the last several years that she had little tolerance
for alcohol, and a huge tolerance for stupidity after a
couple of drinks.

Samantha instantly spied her sister, sitting alone, her
gaze trained out the window next to her. As Samantha
made her way toward her, she realized Melissa had
changed little over the past six years.

Her hair was still pale blond, cut short to emphasize
her dainty features and large eyes. Clad in a beautiful
long-sleeved dress, Melissa looked as if she belonged
in the elegant surroundings.

Samantha tamped down an edge of old childhood resentment. Melissa had often served as their father's
hostess at parties and dinners. She'd displayed a natural
poise and refined deportment, and that, coupled with her
prettiness, had made her Jamison's favorite.

"Why can't you be more like your sister?" How
many times had those words been thrown in Samantha's
face by their father? Too numerous to count. Samantha
shoved these thoughts aside as she reached the table.

"Hi, Missy," she said softly, repeating the nickname their mother had used.

Melissa's head whipped around and for a moment an unexpected warmth lit her eyes. "Sammie."

In that second of greeting, they were two little girls again, sisters and best friends. A hundred memories raced through Samantha's head—pleasant memories of togetherness, and love.

"Sit down." Melissa indicated the chair across from her. She took a sip of water and when she looked back at Samantha the warmth in her eyes had disappeared. "So, back in town for less than twenty-four hours and already you're in the eye of a hurricane."

"You mean the Marcola case?" Melissa nodded. "How'd you hear about it so fast?"

"Small town. Tales of your escapades always make their way from one side to the other. I heard about it from the checker in the grocery store this morning."

"This isn't one of my escapades," Samantha replied, aware of the defensive tone in her voice. "This is a job, a cause I believe in."

"You've upset Tyler by taking this case."

Samantha smiled. "I upset Tyler by being alive." She shrugged. "He'll get over it."

"The only reason you took the Marcola case is because Tyler told you not to."

"Is that what Tyler told you?"

Melissa toyed with her water glass. "Tyler told me he didn't want you to take the case. I'm the one who made the final assessment that it's your perverse nature at work." She leaned forward, her gaze hard and intent. "Don't hurt him, Samantha."

Samantha stared at her in surprise. She leaned back in her chair, an edge of resentment sweeping through her. "Hmm, I guess things *have* changed. There was a time you hated Tyler as much as I did. We both thought of him as the interloper, the encroacher."

"You left, Samantha," Melissa replied. "You turned your back and ran as fast as you could from here." She took another sip of her water. "Tyler's been kind to me."

The arrival of the waiter interrupted the conversation. They placed their orders and when the waiter left, a stifling tension rent the air.

Samantha studied Melissa, wondering if her sister had a thing for Tyler; if perhaps that might be what had broken up her marriage. A sick feeling roiled in her stomach as she thought of Tyler and Melissa together. It felt a little like jealousy, but she dismissed it as hunger pangs.

She didn't care who Tyler was with, as long as it wasn't her. She frowned as she remembered their conversation earlier. The slightly flirtatious nature of their talk had stimulated her, excited her. Again she'd had the feeling of depths unplumbed where Tyler Sinclair was concerned.

Fantasies. If Tyler entertained them at all, she had a feeling his revolved around perfect clients who paid on time or perhaps a little woman who would iron his shirts just the way he liked them.

She snapped her attention back to her sister, irritated that Tyler could so easily sneak into her thoughts. "I understand you've recently separated from your husband," she said.

Melissa's eyes darkened painfully as she nodded. "Although Bill isn't happy about the situation. He doesn't want a divorce."

"What do you want?" Samantha asked.

Melissa unfolded her linen napkin and carefully placed it in her lap. When she looked back at Samantha, her eyes were still darkened by inner shadows. "I don't know. Some days I know the separation is for the best, and then Bill will call and sweet-talk me and I'm not sure if it's right or not. Being alone is so hard." Melissa laughed with an edge of bitterness. "But of course, you probably don't know about that. You've always seemed very comfortable being alone."

Samantha said nothing, although Melissa's words couldn't have been more wrong. She'd never been happy in her aloneness, which was why she'd so often sought the cemetery and the nonjudgmental company of Jeb. But, that was a vulnerability she couldn't expose to anyone, not even Melissa.

"Where are you living?" Samantha asked.

"A little apartment on the north side of town," Melissa replied.

"Why not the house, Melissa? Why didn't you just move home when you separated?"

Melissa shrugged. "Moving back home felt like going backward. I needed time to think, to decide what I want. I didn't want to be influenced by anyone."

The waiter appeared with their lunch. A large salad and iced tea for Melissa and a burger and fries for Samantha.

As they ate, the tension between them eased somewhat. The conversation turned lighter as Melissa filled her in on harmless local gossip. "Margaret Bromswell still drinks too many martinis at community functions and ends the night by singing arias from *Carmen*. Mr. Watkins still wears that horrible toupee, and Bertha Hinke still fixes that awful chicken salad for every potluck dinner she's invited to."

Samantha laughed and stabbed a golden fry with her fork. "I guess some things never change."

Melissa's smile faded and her delicate brow creased with a frown. "Some things have changed. Father's dead."

Samantha nodded. "And we need to decide what to do with the house. You want to sell?"

"I don't know. Things are so unsettled right now in my life. Can we just let things ride for a month or two, then make a decision?" Melissa asked.

"That's fine with me," Samantha agreed. She paused a moment, wanting to broach another subject, but aware that it was an unpleasant one. "Melissa, I intend to investigate Father's death."

Melissa's eyes flared in surprise. "Why? What's to investigate?"

"Don't you find it odd that a man who hated heights, a man who'd lost his wife by a fall from a balcony, would go out on that same balcony and fall through a rotting railing?"

"I find a lot of things odd," Melissa returned, her voice uneven. "I find it odd that the person most likely to break a law has now become a lawyer. I also find it particularly odd that you wanted to meet me for lunch after six years of silence."

Melissa dabbed her mouth with her napkin and refused to meet Samantha's surprised gaze. "Who knows what was going on in Father's mind the night he fell?" she continued.

"But what if he didn't fall?" Samantha countered. "What if he was pushed?"

Melissa looked at her, shadows once again darkening the blue depths of her eyes. "Why would you even think such a thing?"

"Why not?" Samantha retorted. "Father wasn't exactly a beloved figure in this town. I'm sure he had more than a few enemies."

"I'm sure he did," Melissa agreed. "But I can't see any of them sneaking into the house and chasing Father out onto the balcony, then pushing him to his death."

Samantha shook her head. "I don't know what happened. All I know is that something isn't right, and I intend to investigate, find out if it was really an accident or not."

Melissa placed her napkin on the table next to her. "Why can't you just let things rest? You've already entangled yourself in the Marcola mess. Isn't that enough controversy for you?"

"I don't find defending an innocent man against false charges controversial," Samantha replied, her voice cool against the resentment in Melissa's.

Melissa stood. "Samantha, my life contains enough turmoil right now with my marital problems. I don't need you poking and prodding, stirring up things about Father's death."

"Don't you want to know the truth?" Samantha demanded.

"The truth is I think you should sell your half of Justice Inc. to Tyler. He worked for it, he deserves it. The truth is, I think Dominic Marcola would be better off with any other lawyer than you, because when the going gets tough, you have a tendency to run." She paused to draw a breath.

"Gee, it's nice to be home," Samantha said sarcastically.

Melissa flushed. "I'm sorry. I didn't mean to say all that. I've got to go. I told the waiter to put the meal on my tab when I made the reservation. I'll talk to you later.''

Samantha didn't say a word to stop her sister as she turned and walked away. She finished her coffee, ignoring the curious glances of the matrons at their nearby table.

On some level she was unsurprised by Melissa's explosion of anger toward her. While Melissa had never, ever breathed a hint of any resentment she might harbor against her older sister, there had been times before Samantha had left home when she'd felt that emotion simmering just beneath the surface in her sibling.

What she hadn't understood then and what she didn't understand now was why Melissa resented her. What had happened? What had caused the chasm to widen between them, when they'd once been so close?

As she replayed Melissa's words in her mind, an overwhelming sadness descended over her. She'd hoped they would be able to rebuild what they'd once shared in their childhood, the family closeness they'd experienced when their mother was still alive.

Too late. It might be too late for her and Melissa, but it wasn't too late for Samantha to prove both her and Tyler wrong where Dominic was concerned.

She hadn't taken Dominic's case just to be perverse, and she was finished running when things got tough. She threw her napkin on the table and stood. She had too many things to do to sit and ruminate on her problems with Melissa. She had a defense case to prepare and in the process perhaps she could redeem herself in the eyes of her sister and Tyler Sinclair.

Within fifteen minutes she walked into the offices of Justice Inc. for the second time since returning to Wilford. This time a red-haired older woman occupied the receptionist's desk.

"There's my girl!" the busty, slightly overweight woman exclaimed as she came around the desk and embraced Samantha in a hug and a cloud of perfume.

"Oh, Edie, it's so good to see you again," Samantha told her, returning the hug warmly. Edie Burgess had been Jamison Dark's secretary for as long as Samantha could remember.

It had been Edie who had taken Samantha shopping for her very first bra, Edie who had bought birthday and Christmas gifts for the two motherless girls.

"Let me have a look at you." Edie released her and stepped back, gazing at Samantha with sharp, critical eyes. Her ruby lips curved up into a wide grin. "You're looking just fine, sweetheart."

Samantha laughed. "My hair's a mess and my skirt is too short."

"I wouldn't care if you were bald and naked," Edie replied. "I'm just glad you're finally home where you belong." She took Samantha by the hand and led her to the chair next to her desk. "Here, sit down. We've got years of catching up to do."

Samantha had always been rather amazed that a man as conservative, as stodgy as her father had hired a woman who wore her clothes a little too tight, her lipstick a tad too bright, and had hair the color of bottled flames.

"So, tell me all," Edie demanded as Samantha sank down in the chair next to her. "Nobody has told me if you're married or divorced, in love or brokenhearted."

"None of the above," Samantha replied. Oh, in the past six years there had been dates. She'd enjoyed the company of a fellow law student and had entertained a

brief infatuation with a sexy pizza deliveryman, but neither had lasted long. When the men had tried to deepen
the relationship, introduce intimacy, she'd broken it off.
She had no desire to fall in love, didn't believe in it.
All she wanted was a good time, where she stayed in
control and her emotions didn't get involved.

"There hasn't been time for romance," she said.

"Phooey, I'll tell you like I'm always telling Tyler.
You have to make time for romance. Otherwise you'll
wind up alone...like me." Her ruby lips quivered and
tears welled up in her eyes. "Oh, Samantha, honey, I'm
so sorry about your daddy."

Samantha blinked, disconcerted by the swift change
of topic. Instantaneously, grief welled up in her throat,
pushed against her chest with a suffocating tightness.
She swallowed hard against it, unable to understand
why she would grieve for a man she thought she hated.

Edie fumbled in an oversize purse and withdrew a
handful of tissues. She dabbed at her eyes and laughed
self-consciously. "Goodness me, I didn't mean to do
that." She wiped her eyes again, then patted Samantha's
hand. "Now, what's this I hear about you taking on the
Marcola case?"

"We...we're taking on the Marcola case," Samantha
confirmed. "I'm going to need your help on this, Edie."
She smiled and squeezed the older woman's hand. "As
usual, I think I might be in over my head."

Tyler chewed an antacid tablet, grimacing at the familiar chalky taste. He closed the file he'd been working
on and stretched to unkink tight muscles in his back.

It had been a long day. First the trip to the jail to
oversee Samantha's interview with Dominic, then a

glitch in the case he'd been working on that had required hours of research.

He raked a hand through his hair and checked his watch. After seven. Time to call it a day. He pushed away from his desk and grabbed his coat from the closet, then left his office and started down the stairs to the front door.

"What are you doing here this late?" he asked, surprised to see Edie still at her desk.

"Just catching up on a few things." She smiled. "Seems there aren't enough hours in the day."

"Tell me about it," Tyler said dryly. He looked toward Jamison's office. "Did she go home?"

"She left just a few minutes ago, but I don't think she was going right home." Edie's gaze didn't quite meet his.

"Where'd she go?" Tyler asked.

Edie hesitated and in her pause, warning signals went off in Tyler's head. He leaned over her desk, forcing her to look at him. "Edie, where did Samantha go?" he repeated.

"She said something about going to the Devil's Kitchen." Edie's bottom lip quivered with anxiety. "I tried to stop her, told her that was no place for her to go by herself, but you know Samantha."

Tyler stifled a curse as he raced out of the building and toward his car.

Why in the hell would Samantha go to the Devil's Kitchen? The bar was one of the most disreputable—and dangerous—in town.

As he drove, he tried to ignore the acidic roar of pain in his gut. Damn her. What was she up to? At one time or another, every lowlife in a four-state area seemed to migrate to the Devil's Kitchen. She had to be out of her mind to go there—no matter what her reasons.

The bar was located on the north side of town, surprisingly close to the most desirable housing in Wilford. There had been petitions and community efforts to close the tavern, but it had been there long before the expensive houses and apartments were constructed and was protected by the current zoning laws.

As Tyler parked in the overcrowded lot, he realized Morgan Monroe's apartment was a scant two blocks away. He had a feeling that fact had everything to do with Samantha's presence here.

The Devil's Kitchen was housed in a low, squat building that had been painted black and weathered to a dirty gray. A neon outline of a smiling devil, complete with pitchfork, glowed atop the flat roof.

Smoke and noise greeted him as he pushed open the door. For a moment he stood just inside, waiting for his eyes to adjust to the semidarkness.

The jukebox spewed a raucous tune that couldn't compete with the noise of the crowd. Tyler searched for Samantha amid the din, wondering if he would ever again see so many tattoos in one place.

The veneer of civility Tyler had worked so hard to attain slipped away as old survival instincts and adrenaline replaced it. This was a place from his distant past, a landscape from his nightmares.

He'd once sought out bars like this, wanting to fill himself with the rage and utter lawlessness that reigned in such a place.

He realized that now, in his three-piece suit, with his expensive watch and the scent of money clinging to him, he represented nothing more than a temptation to the other men in the bar. They would peg him an easy mark.

But they would be wrong.

He began to weave his way through the throng of people, his gaze scanning for Samantha as he worked his way toward the back of the room.

A scruffy man bumped him, an intentional jolt to his shoulder. Tyler met his eyes, holding his gaze until the man flushed and looked away. Tyler would be lucky to get out of here in one piece, but if he did, he intended to tear into Samantha for putting herself—and him—in a position of risk.

Apprehension crawled up Tyler's spine as he saw no sign of Samantha in the main area of the bar. He knew she had to be here somewhere; her car had been parked out front. The only place left was a small doorway that led to some sort of back room.

Tyler eyed it in horror. Surely she wasn't in there. His mind filled with all sorts of terrible images—Samantha being assaulted amid crates of liquor... Samantha fighting off one assailant after another until she was too weak to resist any longer. With all the noise, nobody would hear her screams.

Without hesitation, Tyler bolted through the doorway, pulling up short as he heard the sound of Samantha's laughter. He felt himself relax somewhat. If she could laugh, then she was still breathing.

He walked around a stack of cases of liquor and there she was, sitting on a crate, talking to a tall, gaunt man whose face bore the pitted remains of adolescent acne.

"Tyler!" She jumped up from her sitting position at the sight of him. "What are you doing here?"

"Looking for you," he answered tersely.

She gestured toward the tall man next to her. "Tyler,

this is Silas Gorman, better known as Bones. Bones, this is my partner, Tyler Sinclair.''

Bones held out a thin hand, his eyes not quite meeting Tyler's. "Hey, man," he muttered.

"You'll call me if you hear anything?" Samantha asked the tall man.

"Anything for you, Sam." He grinned, exposing a flashy gold front tooth.

Samantha nodded in apparent satisfaction, then turned to leave. Tyler trailed behind, wondering how she knew Mr. Bones...unsure if he really wanted to know.

As she wove her way through the crowd toward the front door, Tyler observed the leering looks she earned from the men she passed. Thank goodness she wasn't wearing one of her short skirts, but rather was clad in a pair of worn jeans and an oversize sweatshirt.

She'd almost reached the front door when a big, burly man grabbed her arm and said something to her. Although Tyler was too far behind to hear what the man had said, he saw her eyes widen as she tried to wrench her arm away from his tight grasp.

"I knew it," Tyler breathed to himself with dread. Somehow he'd known they wouldn't get out of here without one altercation. He shoved forward to where the creep still had hold of Samantha.

"Let the lady go," he demanded.

"Mind your own business," the big man snarled, his breath sour with the odor of too much whiskey and too many cigarettes.

"The lady is my business," Tyler coolly replied as he stepped closer to the man. His ulcer went into overdrive as he realized his opponent was a full head taller than him and outweighed him by at least fifty pounds.

However, the fear in Samantha's face and the slight grimace of pain that twisted her features sent adrenaline surging through Tyler.

"I'm going to tell you one more time, let the lady go. If you don't understand my words, perhaps you'll understand a more direct form of communication," Tyler warned.

The big man's eyes flared, as if he found the idea of a brawl with Tyler fun. He let go of Samantha's arm and turned to face Tyler. His nostrils flared, like those of a bull ready to charge. Tyler saw the punch coming and easily sidestepped the swing. The creep roared in rage and came back with a left jab that glanced off Tyler's jaw.

Tyler was vaguely aware of Samantha's scream, but he ignored it, focusing completely on his antagonist. The two men warily circled each other, with shouts of encouragement coming from the spectators nearby.

Nobody seemed inclined to either call the police or step in to help and Tyler only hoped that if he managed to punch the guy out, another wouldn't take his place.

"Take him, Brennon!" a voice shouted.

"Yeah, dirty his suit, Rick!" another yelled.

Rick Brennon. At least Tyler would know the name of the man who pounded him. He hoped when Rick Brennon got through with him, he would remember that Samantha had gotten him into this mess.

Still, Tyler didn't intend to go down easy. He'd grown up on the dark side of St. Louis, fighting creeps like Rick Brennon in an effort to stay alive.

His breath caught in his throat as a knife suddenly appeared in Brennon's hand. "Come on, pretty boy," Brennon taunted him. "Come get a taste of this."

Tyler eyed him in disgust. "What's the matter? Afraid to face me without that steel in your hand?"

Brennon's eyes narrowed as he barked a laugh. He tossed the knife to a fat man standing nearby, then gestured Tyler closer. "Bring it on, pretty boy."

Knowing there was no way he was going to get out of here without a fight, Tyler drew strength from the rush that eddied through him. Biding his time, he waited for Brennon to attack. When he did, Tyler responded.

In three swift moves, Tyler had Brennon on his back on the floor, and his foot pressed against Brennon's thick throat. "An honorable man would let this end right here," he said, his voice low and dangerous. "A stupid man would continue until one of us is bloody and bowed. Personally, it's going to tick me off if I get blood on my suit. So, are you going to be honorable or stupid?"

Brennon's eyes flickered his answer and Tyler removed his foot. As the big man got to his feet, Tyler grabbed Samantha by the arm and hurried her toward the door.

"Get in my car," he said when they were outside.

"What about my car?" she asked.

"We'll come back for it."

"But—"

"Samantha, get in the damn car before I really lose my temper and toss you back inside that place."

She obviously recognized the threat as possible. Almost meekly, she opened his passenger door and slid inside. Tyler got behind the wheel. Now that the imminent danger had passed, the surge of survival instinct waned, leaving behind only a heady anger directed at the woman beside him.

"Tyler, I—"

"Samantha, do yourself a favor. Don't say anything for the moment." He started the car and pulled out of the parking lot. "In a few minutes I'm going to ask you why I shouldn't wrap my hands around your pretty little throat." He glared at her balefully. "You might take this quiet time to be thinking of reasons why I shouldn't."

Chapter 5

Samantha knew Tyler was mad as hell. His knuckles were white as he gripped the steering wheel. She had a feeling he envisioned the wheel as her neck. She cleared her throat, a wave of heat cascading through her as she thought of those hands, not tight around her neck but instead, languidly stroking.

She straightened and diverted the heat vent that had been blowing hot air in her face. She didn't know what he was so mad about. Everything probably would have been fine had he not interfered. But, she had a feeling that mentioning this particular fact might be a big mistake.

They were nearly home when he finally spoke. "Now, you want to tell me why on earth you went to that place?" His tone was measured—controlled calm.

"The night Abigail Monroe was murdered, the anonymous 911 call was made from the Devil's Kitchen." She hesitated a moment, then continued. "Don't you find it strange that somebody ran two blocks to make a call that a woman was in danger in apartment 502?"

Tyler remained silent, his brow pulled into a thoughtful frown.

Samantha turned in her seat to face him. "I think the real killer made that call, knowing Dominic was passed out on the bed and would be charged with the crime."

"And did you expect the culprit to be standing by the phone this evening?" Tyler asked dryly.

"Of course not," Samantha retorted, irritated that he made her feel foolish. "I went there tonight to ask some questions, find out if anyone knew anything about Abigail Monroe's murder. Sometimes alcohol loosens lips and bragging becomes an art form, especially in places like the Devil's Kitchen."

"How do you know Bones?" He pulled into the driveway and cut the engine.

"Why don't we finish this conversation inside?" she suggested. She would feel better talking in the house, where she could gain some safe distance between them. She wasn't fooled by his outward composure. Anger still sparkled in his eyes and she was far too aware of her close proximity to him.

As they got out of the car and went into the house, Samantha followed behind him, remembering how easily Tyler had taken down Rick Brennon. It shocked her that Tyler had so smoothly overwhelmed the bigger, meaner opponent and hadn't even broken into a sweat.

For the first time since Tyler had entered her life so many years before, curiosity about his life before the Darks entered her mind.

Virginia met them at the kitchen door, her face as usual radiating dour disapproval as she eyed Samantha.

"There's ham and scalloped potatoes in the refrigerator and a loaf of homemade bread in the bin."

"Sounds delicious," Samantha said, realizing she was ravenous.

"Hmm, it was delicious two hours ago." Virginia plucked her coat from the back of a kitchen chair and pulled it on. "I'll just be on my way," she said. With a curt nod to them both, she turned and left.

"I never understood why Father hired Virginia," Samantha said when the older woman had gone. "She's the most sour woman I've ever known."

"She was utterly devoted to your father for many years." Tyler sat down at the table. "He left her a small stipend in his will, but she wanted to continue to work, so I've kept her on here."

Samantha walked to the refrigerator and pulled out the items Virginia had prepared for their dinner. She could tell Tyler was still angry. Muscles had formed a knot at his jaw and he slowly thrummed his fingers on the tabletop as if mentally ticking off ways to punish her. Tension filled the air, as thick and rich as the scalloped potatoes she spooned onto her plate.

"Hungry?" she asked in an attempt to dispel some of the tension.

He eyed her balefully. "I lost my appetite about the same time I realized I was going to have to fight Goliath to get you safely out of the bar."

Samantha filled two plates and shoved them into the oversize microwave. "You have to eat." She turned back to face Tyler. "I must admit, you surprised me with your smooth moves. Where'd you learn how to fight?"

A dark eyebrow crooked upward in an expression of dry amusement. He stopped the movement of fingers against the table. "Contrary to what you believe, I wasn't born and raised in a three-piece suit on the conservative side of the law."

"Where *were* you born and raised?" It was odd that she'd never asked before. In all the time he'd been a part of the family, she'd never asked him any personal questions about his life before the Darks.

"St. Louis. I lived there until your father sent me to college."

She looked at him in surprise. "How did you meet my father?"

He leaned back in the chair and Samantha could almost see the tension leaving him as he relaxed. "I was a junior when your father came to our high school as a guest speaker in my civics class." Tyler's eyes softened at the memory. "He was the most dynamic man I'd ever met. He exuded power, control—all the things I didn't have in my life at the time." He smiled. "Your father could be a very charismatic man when he wanted."

She nodded, then placed silverware on the table. "So he came to talk to your class. That doesn't explain how you came to be his protégé."

The smile remained on Tyler's face. "There was a question-and-answer period after his talk. Jamison later told me I was the only one who asked intelligent questions and that he could see ambition burning in my eyes."

"And so he offered to mentor you," Samantha finished, wishing her father had been able to look deeper than her acts of rebellion to see her burning need for him. Tyler nodded. "What about your parents? What did they think?"

He shifted positions. His smile faded as he rubbed

his stomach. "I never knew my father. He left my mom when she was seven months pregnant and we never heard from him again. My mother died when I was fourteen."

Sympathy battled with guilt inside Samantha. She knew well the pain of losing a mother at a young age and imagined the trauma was just as great for him at fourteen as it had been for her at six. In all the time she'd cursed and resented Tyler's presence in their life, she'd never considered the possibility that he had no other family of his own. "I'm sorry, Tyler," she said softly. "Was it an illness, or some sort of accident?"

He drew a deep breath and raked a hand through his hair, his eyes radiating a darkness, a kind of pain that almost frightened Samantha. She wondered if perhaps she had stepped over a line, intruded too far into his privacy.

The microwave dinged and she jumped. The darkness lifted from his eyes and he cast her a tight smile. "I've been a part of your life for almost fifteen years and you've never displayed any kind of curiosity about me. Why the interest now?"

She set a plate in front of him, then placed hers opposite him at the table and sat down. "At the moment, I like you better than I ever have." She grinned at his frown. "Don't worry. I'm sure the feeling will pass very quickly."

An answering smile touched his lips. It was a real smile, not the derisive kind she'd come to expect from him. As an unexpected warmth shot through her, she lowered her gaze and focused on her plate.

She ate, not tasting the food, trying to get back her equilibrium where he was concerned. She was sorry she'd asked him about his family. It was far easier to keep emotional distance without the complication of empathy.

Tyler seemed lost in his own thoughts, his brow furrowed as he ate methodically. For the first time in years, Samantha allowed herself to mentally replay the night she'd tried to seduce him.

As usual, she'd left the house after fighting with her father. She no longer remembered what the fight had been about; she only remembered the reckless hurt and anger that had driven her to the James Tavern, where she'd proceeded to drink herself silly.

She hadn't known it at the time, but the bartender was an old client of her father's. He'd made a phone call and Tyler had been dispatched to retrieve the recalcitrant Samantha.

Tyler's arrival at the bar had only incensed her even more. Her father hadn't cared enough to come himself, but rather had sent his underling.

Disgust had tightened Tyler's features as he'd taken her arm and led her out of the bar. His disapproval shouted in his utter silence as they got into his car. Somehow, Samantha's anger had twisted inside her, battling with the underlying attraction she'd always felt for him.

In the close confines of his car, with the scent of his provocative cologne filling the air, the desire Samantha had fought against for so long surfaced without the usual inhibitions. Along with desire came simple need—the need to be held, to be loved.

She'd scooted next to him and placed her hand on his thigh. His reaction was instantaneous. She heard his swift intake of breath, felt the tightening of muscles that implied a desire of his own.

There had been no triumph in the knowledge that he

might want her, only a quickening of her heart. She'd leaned against him, brushing his jaw with her lips, wishing only that for a few minutes he would make her feel loved, cherished.

"Samantha?"

Jerked from her thoughts of the past, she felt heat wash over her face in a blush as she looked at him. "What?" she asked, hoping her features revealed nothing of her memories.

"You have to make me a promise." His dark blue, mesmerizing eyes held hers for a long moment.

"What kind of promise?"

"Promise me you won't do something stupid like you did tonight. Promise me you won't go anywhere near the Devil's Kitchen or any place like that again."

"I can't do that." Samantha broke their eye contact, uncomfortable as she tried to shove aside her memories of wanting him, of needing him. "I have to go wherever my investigation takes me, wherever I might find proof of Dominic's innocence."

Tyler stood and took his empty plate to the sink. "I'll give Wylie Brooks a call tomorrow, see if I can talk him out of his retirement to give you a hand," he said as he rinsed his plate and stuck it in the dishwasher. He turned back to face her. "In the meantime, would you at least promise me you won't go anywhere alone? If you need to investigate away from the office, tell me and I'll go with you."

"I thought you didn't want to be involved in this in any way," Samantha reminded.

"I didn't," he replied. "But I can't in good conscience allow you to stumble around, stirring up trouble and putting yourself at risk."

"Let me guess. It's bad for the reputation of the firm," she replied with a touch of sarcasm.

"Exactly." He looked as if he were about to say something more but instead raked a hand through his hair and sighed tiredly. "Are you planning on attending the funeral tomorrow?"

She nodded. Abigail Monroe would be laid to rest the following day. "Who knows, maybe the real killer will break down and throw himself across her casket."

He smiled. "Things like that only happen in the movies." His smile faded. "I have a feeling there will be no Perry Mason moments in this case. Just hard work and heartache." He eyed her thoughtfully. "For your sake I hope you're up to it."

"For Dominic's sake, I have to be." She raised her chin a notch in determination.

Although she knew she looked strong and decisive, her insides quivered in fear. She was scared—scared that she would prove her father right, her sister right. She'd always made a mess of things, but in the past the consequences had always been hers alone to endure.

She felt as if this was her last chance to prove something not only to Tyler and Melissa and the rest of the people of Wilford, but also to herself. She was intensely aware that this time if she messed up, she wouldn't be the only one to carry the burden. Dominic would wind up on death row, and Samantha had a feeling she would spiral so out of control she would never find her way back.

The funeral for Abigail Monroe nearly shut down all the businesses in Wilford. Store owners and workers stopped for the afternoon to attend and pay their respects not so much to the dead, but rather to the powerful man she'd been married to.

Samantha got out of her car, grateful she'd opted for black slacks instead of a dress as a cold autumn breeze greeted her, slapping her in the face and cutting through the suede jacket she wore. Although it was only late September, the air held more than a hint of early winter.

It was just two in the afternoon and she was already exhausted. Dominic's arraignment had been that morning. Samantha hadn't been surprised, but nevertheless was disappointed that she hadn't managed to talk Judge Halloran into setting reasonable bail.

The cemetery was already filled with people as Samantha picked her way through the other grave sites to where a large tent structure had been erected. Low whispers filled the tent, along with the cloying scent of floral wreaths and sprays.

Next to the flower-bedecked white casket, Morgan Monroe sat in a chair, surrounded by friends and family.

At the moment Morgan didn't look like a crazed killer; he looked like a grieving old man. His face was colorless, his eyes red-rimmed. Samantha had already checked Morgan's alibi. As Tyler had told her, it appeared airtight. But, that didn't mean he hadn't hired somebody to take care of the murder for him.

Next to him stood a young man with similar physical characteristics, although the strong features showed no signs of grief. A son, Samantha guessed, mentally adding him to the list of potential suspects.

She tried not to think about the fact that her father was buried nearby. Perhaps eventually she would want to take flowers to his grave. At the moment, she didn't feel mentally prepared to say her final goodbyes to the man who had so ruled her life and dictated her choices; a man who had never found a reason to love her.

"Samantha?"

Samantha turned toward the feminine voice coming from behind her. "Marcia? Marcia Wise?"

The petite brunette grinned. "It's Marcia Wellington now. I married Dennis right after graduation."

Samantha remembered Dennis Wellington, one of the star football players on the Wilford Tigers team. Marcia had been a cheerleader and although not particularly close to Samantha, had always been friendly. "I heard you were in town. It's good to have you back."

Samantha grinned at her old high-school acquaintance. "You're one of the few who think it's nice I'm back."

"Some turnout, huh?" Marcia gestured toward the crowd.

"Were you a friend of Abigail's?" Samantha asked curiously.

Marcia shook her head. "Not really. I'd seen her around town, but we didn't know each other personally. Dennis works at the bank for Mr. Morgan. He's working now, but I thought it would be a good idea if I came and paid my respects."

"Looks like the whole town thought it would be a good idea," Samantha observed as she scanned the large group of people.

"It's almost as big a turnout as when your father was buried." Marcia touched Samantha's arm lightly. "I'm sorry for your recent loss."

"Thanks."

For a moment the two were silent, each scanning the crowd. Samantha wasn't surprised that her father's funeral had drawn a huge turnout. Jamison Jackson Dark

had been a man every bit as powerful and respected as
Morgan Monroe.

"Samantha, I heard you're representing Dominic."

"That's right," Samantha replied.

"Dennis and I are good friends of his. I don't care
how bad it looks, I know he couldn't have killed Abigail
under any circumstances. He loved her."

Samantha nodded. "I feel the same way, and I intend
to do everything in my power to see that the truth comes
out." It felt good to hear somebody else voice support
for Dominic, and utter disbelief that he could have been
involved in such a crime.

Samantha stiffened as she saw Tyler standing on the
opposite side of the tent. She hadn't seen him or spoken
to him since last night. He'd gone up to his room while
she still sat at the table, finishing her meal along with
trying to swallow her fears.

His head was bent as he listened to a petite woman
standing next to him. He looked achingly handsome in
a three-quarter-length black trench coat belted at his
slender waist.

As he flashed the attractive blonde a smile, a fury of
resentment swelled inside Samantha. He certainly had
never smiled at her like that, so openly friendly. His
smiles for Samantha were always laced with overt arrogance and mockery.

"He's quite a hunk, isn't he?"

Samantha grimaced, realizing that Marcia had followed her gaze and was speaking about Tyler. "He's
all right," she answered grudgingly.

"All right? I'd say most of the women in town have
wicked fantasies about Mr. All Right over there." Marcia laughed. "If I wasn't so happily married, I'd jump
his bones in a minute."

Samantha was grateful the minister chose that moment to begin the graveside services and there was no further opportunity for idle chatter about Tyler.

Still, as the minister continued his sermon, Samantha found her thoughts wandering back to that distant night when she'd sat so close to Tyler, had needed him to hold her, tell her she was good and valuable. Instead he had pushed her away, scorn darkening his eyes—the same scorn she'd always seen in her father's eyes.

She drew her collar up around her neck, chilled once again by thoughts of that night of humiliation. Had she succeeded in seducing him and they had made love, he would have been shocked to discover that the "bad girl" of Wilford, Kansas, was in actuality a virgin.

Samantha knew that Tyler, like her father, had always assumed the worst about her, including the belief that she'd enjoyed a wild sexual freedom.

Nothing could be further from the truth. Oh, she'd snuck out of the house, met boys with bad reputations. She'd dated often, deliberately choosing boys she knew her father would hate.

She'd been caught skinny-dipping in the park, and had nearly surrendered her virginity to Larry, a boy with soulful eyes who'd professed he would love her till the end of time. Ultimately she'd told Larry that if he really loved her he would wait until she was ready, and apparently, for Larry, that had been "the end of time." He'd broken up with her that same night.

Since Larry, there had been no other man with whom she'd felt any kind of heart-searing, mind-numbing passion. Until Tyler.

It irritated and angered her that the one man she didn't want anything to do with had the capacity to make her think of tangled sheets and bare skin, hot hands and heated sighs.

She tore her gaze from him, trying to focus her thoughts on the minister's final farewell to Abigail Monroe. She didn't want to think about Tyler. She needed to watch the crowd, check for inappropriate or unusual reactions. She had a feeling that whoever was actually responsible for Abigail's death was probably here, saying a personal final goodbye.

The service was brief. Afterward, people milled around as if reluctant to return to their jobs or their lives. Samantha stood off to one side, watching as people approached Morgan Monroe and his son. Morgan accepted the words of comfort and sympathy with a barely contained dignity, looking as if at any moment he would shatter into a hundred pieces.

"Counselor, I'm rather surprised to see you here."

Samantha hid a grimace of distaste behind a smile as she greeted the assistant district attorney, the man she would be facing in Dominic's trial and had sparred with that morning at the arraignment. "Chester."

She acknowledged his presence with a dip of her head.

Chester Sparks had been a peer of her father's, although Jamison had had nothing but derision for the dapper dresser with his penchant for outrageous ties.

Chester liked to think of himself as a ladies' man. He had three ex-wives and chased everything in skirts. The salacious look he gave Samantha should have earned him a sound slap. "You're a mighty little thing to be trying to fill your daddy's shoes," he said as he sidled close enough to her that she could smell the scent of his deodorant.

She took a step back from him. "I have unusually big feet," she retorted.

He laughed, his hazel eyes sparking with a presumptuous intimacy that made Samantha's skin crawl. "I'm looking forward to battling you in the courtroom. I've always found a good intellectual contest sexually stimulating. What about you?"

"There you are." Tyler's smooth voice came from behind her.

He stepped next to her and took her arm. He nodded curtly to Chester, then smiled at Samantha. "I've been looking all over for you. We've got to get back to the office."

"That man should be arrested," Samantha fumed as Tyler led her out of the tent.

Tyler released his hold on her arm and laughed. "Unfortunately, being a buffoon isn't considered a crime."

"His taste in ties should at least make him guilty of a misdemeanor," she replied. She stopped walking. "Thanks for the rescue. Another minute or two and you'd have been representing *me* on a murder charge."

"I could tell by the look in your eyes that he was getting to you."

"I remember Dad used to say if snakes wore ties they'd all be named Chester."

Tyler laughed and Samantha felt a sweeping warmth suffuse her at the pleasant sound. The afternoon sun played on his hair, glinting on reddish highlights that were normally invisible. The cold wind had whipped color into his cheeks, but Samantha suspected that despite the coolness of the breeze his skin would be warm.

She averted her gaze from him, wondering why on earth he affected her on such a primal level. People were starting to head toward their cars and Samantha's attention was caught by one particular woman, clad all in black. Her face displayed deep grief as tears rolled down her cheeks.

"Tyler, who is that woman?" Samantha asked.

Tyler followed her gaze, then looked back at Samantha. "Georgia Morgan. The first Mrs. Morgan."

"Why on earth is she so distraught?"

Tyler shrugged. "I think Georgia and Abigail had become friends."

Samantha watched as the woman fumbled in her purse and withdrew a tissue, then got into her car. Another name to add to her growing list of suspects. She suddenly had the feeling of time passing—and wasting. Dominic's case would begin in less than two weeks and Samantha had only started her investigation.

She looked back at Tyler. "Thanks again for the rescue. I've got to get to the office. There's a ton of work waiting for me."

As she got in her car she cast one last look at Tyler. The trench coat flapped against the length of his legs and the wind tousled his hair. God, he was such a handsome man.

She had to remember that he was her adversary. He'd come into their lives and stolen her father's love from her. He'd wiggled his way to a place in her father's heart that Samantha had been denied. He'd even finagled half of Justice Inc. for himself.

For years she'd believed she hated him, had wanted to hate him; but she found that particular, comforting emotion difficult to evoke at this moment, and that frightened her.

Tyler had always made it very clear he thought little of her and the last thing she wanted was to entertain any warm, fuzzy feelings for him. That was the formula for heartache and she'd had enough of that while growing up. She'd long ago decided never to allow a man access to her heart, and she refused to let Tyler be an exception to that rule.

As she pulled away from the cemetery, she buried any desire she might have for Tyler deep in her heart, where hopefully it would rest in peace forever, never to be retrieved.

Chapter 6

For the third time in as many minutes Tyler shifted position against the mattress that suddenly felt too hard, too lumpy for sleep.

Usually sleep came easily for him, but tonight he'd been tossing and turning for the past hour. Giving up, he swung his legs over the side of the bed and stood. A hollow pain gnawed at his stomach and he pressed a hand against it as he reached for his robe.

It had been months since he'd had an ulcer flare-up this intense and he knew exactly what had caused this latest eruption. Samantha.

He'd spent the last two days at Justice Inc., hearing the sounds of merriment drifting up the stairs from Jamison's office. Samantha's laughter, vibrant and melodic, filled the entire building. She and Edie and Miranda, the filing clerk, had holed up in Jamison's luxurious room like the plotting Three Musketeers.

Tyler had a feeling Samantha had enlisted the others'

aid in the investigation for the Marcola case, and that worried him. That was all she needed—an airhead receptionist and a giggling file clerk as her support team. He made a mental note to contact Wylie Brooks first thing in the morning and convince the private eye to come out of retirement for this particular case.

Yanking on his robe, he left his room and went downstairs to the study. The fire had nearly died, leaving behind the glow of hot embers.

He added a log from the stack in the corner, then prodded with the poker until flames danced, licking hungrily at the new, dry wood. He set the poker down and stared at the fire, absently rubbing his stomach.

"Thanks, I was too lazy to get up and add a log."

He jumped in surprise and turned to see Samantha curled up in one of the wing chairs in front of the fireplace. "You scared the hell out of me," he exclaimed.

"Sorry." She flashed a small smile. "I thought you saw me here and just didn't feel like talking."

With the light from the fire, he could see her clearly. Curled up and clad in a navy robe, without makeup and with her hair a tumbling mass of curls, she looked soft and vulnerable.

He turned on a table lamp and strode over to the bar. Grabbing the bottle of brandy, he tried to ignore the ache in his stomach.

"You'd be better off with a glass of milk," she observed. "What is it? An ulcer?"

He eyed her in surprise and realized he was once again rubbing his stomach. He grimaced, displeased that she'd noticed and had guessed what ailed him. To him, the ulcer implied a weakness, a lack of control over his emotions and body.

Nodding, he splashed brandy in the bottom of a glass,

then walked back toward the fire and sat down in the chair opposite hers. "Milk would probably be better, but I prefer brandy."

She smiled. "And they call me perverse. How long have you had it?"

"Two years. Since *Waltrip* v. *Burlington*."

"Bad case?" she asked.

"The case wasn't so tough—a real-estate deal gone bad. But the litigants were both horrid. It was the first and only time I was found in contempt because of my client's outrageous outbursts. Judge Halloran wasn't amused."

"He a tough judge?"

Tyler sipped his drink before answering. "Tough, but fair."

"He wasn't too bad at the arraignment."

Tyler nodded. "Just remember he's the boss of his courtroom and you'll do fine with him." He eyed her curiously. "Why did you go into law, Samantha?"

She shifted positions, flashing a long length of leg before covering up again with the robe. "Why not?" She smiled ruefully. "I know why you're surprised. With my rebellious nature you expected me to do—to be something a little less conventional. Like maybe an exotic dancer, or a stripper."

Tyler's head instantly filled with a vision of her on a stage, clad in a sparkly G-string and a tiny top that scarcely hid her lush breasts.

He tightened his grip on his glass as his stomach burned and his groin tightened. "You have to admit, when you left here you weren't exactly on the fast track to success."

"No, I was a mess." She sighed and turned her attention to the fire.

Her admission surprised him. He studied her features, highlighted by the golden flames. What streak of perversity existed in him that found her so fascinating? She was pretty, but as an eligible, successful lawyer, Tyler could have his pick of the pretty women in town.

No, it wasn't so much the way she looked that had captured Tyler. It was her passion, her simmering anger that drew him. It was her thought process, and the actions that resulted from it that had always intrigued him.

But it was an intrigue, an attraction he didn't intend to follow through on. Somehow, he feared that Samantha would be as destructive to him as the anger and passion that had once ruled him and he had since learned to tame.

"Father always expected the worst from me, and so that's what I gave him. It wasn't until I left here—left him—that I began to expect more from myself." She looked back at him, returning to his initial question. "Why not the law? It was what I knew, what I'd grown up with." She flashed him a wicked grin. "Besides, it's far less respectable than stripping for a living." She sobered, her gaze holding his. "You don't like me very much, do you?"

Again she managed to take him by surprise, this time with her directness, her utter lack of guile. "I don't think I liked you much when you were a teenager," he answered truthfully. "The jury is still out on whether I like the woman you've become."

She nodded, as if expecting no more, no less from him.

"We don't have to like each other to work together."

"Who knows? Maybe we'll learn to like each other, given enough time."

She laughed. "You'd have to loosen up a bit before that could happen."

He returned her smile. "And you'd have to straighten up a bit."

For a moment, an amicable camaraderie flowed between them. The fire snapped and crackled cheerfully as the flames shot dancing shadows around the room. He leaned back in his chair, his gaze still focused on her.

"It must have been tough, being on your own and putting yourself through law school." As he said the words, unexpected admiration swept through him. For the first time, he considered what her life must have been like for the past six years without the support of family or friends. He finished his brandy and placed the empty glass on the stone hearth.

"It was tough," she agreed. She stared into the fire, and wrapped her arms around herself. "It helped that I had a little money left from my inheritance from Mom. That got me through the first year. Then I worked at a variety of part-time jobs while I finished school."

Tyler shook his head. "It's funny. Law school would have been out of the question for me without your father. He did for me what you refused to let him do for you."

"I didn't refuse anything," she countered as she looked at him once again. "My father never offered me anything but criticism. Sometimes I think I made it through law school just to spite him."

Tyler laughed. "Now that sounds like the Samantha Dark I know."

Silence fell between them as they both stared into the fire. Tyler realized that at some point during the last few minutes his stomach had quit hurting. Who would have thought he and Samantha could have a rational, almost-pleasant conversation?

He cast her a surreptitious glance, surprised to see a glimmer of tears in her eyes. "Samantha?" He leaned forward, unsure of what he was seeing.

She sniffed and swiped at her eyes with an embarrassed laugh. "Sorry. It crept up on me with no warning." She drew a deep breath and once again wrapped her arms around her shoulders as if to ward off a chill.

"You sure you're okay?" Tyler asked tentatively.

She turned and looked at him, her eyes luminous. "I just can't believe he's gone." To his horror, she burst into tears.

In all the years Tyler had been a part of the Dark family, he'd never seen Samantha cry. It shook him, this sudden exposure to a side of her he'd never considered—a soft vulnerability he hadn't known she possessed.

Up until now, he hadn't been sure she'd even been touched by her father's death. She'd shed no tears that he knew of, hadn't been to the cemetery, had scarcely spoken of the man who had been her father.

He sat for a moment, unsure what to do, how to respond. Her grief shocked him. He hadn't expected it from her—not for the man she'd seemed to hate for so long.

When her tears showed no sign of abatement, he got up and approached her, wanting to comfort, but unsure how.

Before he could reach her, she stood and walked into his arms, spilling her grief on the front of his robe. Her scent surrounded him. Her hair smelled of tropical flowers, the fragrance mingling with the subtle spicy perfume she always wore.

Tentatively he wrapped his arms around her, awkwardly patting her back as she continued to cry. "It's going to be all right," he murmured, wishing he knew better words to say to bring comfort.

He was a lawyer. Lawyers were supposed to be men of many words, but all the phrases that sprang to his mind sounded like empty, meaningless platitudes.

He opted for silence, merely holding her and soothing her back with his hand as her body shook with the force of her sobs.

She didn't cry hard for long. Within minutes her sobs lessened in intensity, becoming gasps for control. Still she didn't move from his embrace, but rather seemed to burrow closer against his chest, as if soothed by the warmth of his body.

Within moments his pats on her back became caresses, her silk robe slick and sensuous beneath his hands.

The closeness of her body warmed his and he felt a stir of desire ripple through him. He fought against it, not wanting to want her. She turned her head away from his chest and her breath was warm against the side of his neck as her crying finally ceased.

Tyler knew he should move away from her, step away from the arms that clung around his neck, away from the body that pressed so close against his.

He wondered what she wore beneath the silky robe. It felt as if there was nothing between the robe and the heat of her skin.

She probably slept naked, he thought, torturing himself with erotic visions of her in bed wearing nothing but her damnable sexy smile.

His arms tightened around her even as he realized the danger of his thoughts. She tilted her head to look up at him, her lips parted as if awaiting his kiss. Her eyes were the color of dark chocolate, imploring him, enticing him.

Just as he'd known with weary resignation that he wouldn't escape the Devil's Kitchen without a fight, he knew there was no way he wasn't going to kiss Samantha. Someplace in the back of his mind, he had the fleeting hope that in kissing her once, he would sate his hunger for her and be done with her once and for all.

Tentatively he touched his lips to hers, unsurprised to find hers moist and welcoming. He'd intended to keep the kiss light, controlled, but the moment she opened her mouth to him, he abdicated all thoughts of control.

She tasted of heat and desire, and Tyler wound his fingers in her hair as he deepened the kiss. As his tongue swirled with hers, every nerve in his body came alive with an electric current that crackled through him. All caution, all rational thought left him as he lost himself in her nearness, in the fire of her lips.

As their kiss ended, she tilted her head back, allowing him access to the slender column of her neck. Her breathing came in rapid gasps, letting him know her want was just as powerful as his own.

He pressed his mouth against her dainty earlobe, then kissed down her neck to the hollow of her throat. She trembled in his arms, as if overwhelmed by the force of her response to his every caress. This only heightened Tyler's response.

A low moan escaped him as he moved his hands from her back to the swell of her breasts against her robe. The silk was no longer cool, but rather welcomingly warm, and her nipples pressed against his palms as if seeking escape from the garment.

He pushed her robe off one shoulder, unsurprised to find nothing but sweet-smelling skin. She held the robe closed across her breasts for a long moment as she looked into his eyes.

Tyler remained still, his heart thudding so hard, so loudly he wondered if perhaps she had uttered a protest and he hadn't heard. He stepped back from her, unsure; still filled with desire, but not wanting to take what she didn't want to give.

His breath caught in his chest as she smiled, then shrugged out of the robe, allowing it to fall in a pool of navy silk at her feet. Clad only in a pair of tiny lace panties, with the fire glow painting her in warm golden hues, her loveliness made Tyler ache.

At that moment the window next to where they stood suddenly exploded inward. Samantha screamed as Tyler pulled her down to the floor, unsure what was happening. Through the broken window came the squeal of tires as a car tore away.

Tyler jumped up and raced to the window in time to see the distant flare of taillights just before they disappeared into the darkness of the night. He remained standing there, breathing heavily as his brain tried to shift from desire to response to the threat of danger.

He turned away from the window, carefully trying to avoid the shards of glass that littered the floor.

"What's going on? What happened?" Samantha asked, her voice shaky as she grabbed her robe and belted it tightly around her.

Tyler spied a brick on the floor, apparently the missile that had sailed through the window. He picked it up, surprised to find a message written on it. "It's a note from your fan club," he said to Samantha and held the brick up so she could read what was written there.

"'Drop the Marcola case.'" Samantha frowned. "What kind of nonsense is this?" she exclaimed as she began to pace back and forth in front of the fire.

Tyler watched her in growing irritation. Each step she took exposed a long length of bare leg, making it difficult for him to think, to focus on the matter at hand.

The shattering of the window had come at an opportune time, stopping him from doing something incredibly stupid. "I warned you this had all the earmarks of becoming a volatile case. Perhaps you managed to stir somebody up with your little visit to the Devil's Kitchen. For God's sake, would you sit down?"

Samantha stopped in her tracks, apparently surprised by the sharpness of his tone. She flounced down in the chair and glared up at him. "If you or anyone else thinks a brick through the window will make me drop this case, you're sadly mistaken. If anything, this just makes me more determined. It lets me know somebody is afraid of what I might find out."

Tyler frowned. "Samantha, I wish you would reconsider, let a court-appointed defense counsel handle Dominic's case."

"And I wish you'd sell me your half of Justice Inc.," she countered. "We don't always get what we want."

Tyler narrowed his gaze, wondering if perhaps what had almost happened moments before between them had been an attempt at manipulation on her part. Had she thought that by seducing him he would agree to give her his half of the firm? He shoved this thought from his mind, unable to believe she would be that underhanded.

"Why are you so hell-bent on representing Marcola? Did you and Dominic have a thing at some time in the past?" It was a question that had gnawed at him since she'd announced her intention to represent the suspected murderer.

"Are you having a thing with my sister?"

"Good heavens, no," Tyler replied, shocked at the very suggestion.

"Well, there was never anything between Dominic and me. I guess he's the one man in town I missed having a 'thing' with," she replied sarcastically.

"Besides me, but then you did try with me that night I pulled you out of the James Tavern."

Her reaction to his words was immediate. Her back stiffened and her cheeks flamed red. "That doesn't count. I was drunk and didn't know what I was doing."

"On the contrary, you seemed to know exactly what you were doing, as you once again displayed only moments ago." Tyler knew he was feeding her anger as effectively as he'd fed the fire when he'd first entered the room. He couldn't help it. He felt safer with anger between them.

She rose from her chair and advanced toward him, her cheeks still flaming with bewitching color. She stopped only when she stood mere inches from him. "You don't ever have to worry about me making unwanted advances on you again," she said softly as her breasts rose and fell with uneven breaths. "I'd sleep with Henry Watkins and his ugly toupee before I'd sleep with you."

"That's fine with me," he retorted. "I generally sleep with women I love, and I'm not even sure I like you very much."

She stepped back from him. "I don't intend to lose any sleep over whether you like me or not."

"I don't expect you to. What should give you sleepless nights is that if you mess up Dominic's defense, he faces the death penalty.''

Her eyes darkened. "Don't you think I know that? What should give you sleepless nights is that when I win Dominic's case, I'll be the number-one lawyer in Justice Inc., and I won't be happy until I force you out." She whirled around and stomped out of the room. Tyler heard the angry tread of her footsteps as she climbed the stairs to the bedrooms.

"Call the police," he called after her. "We need to make a report of this."

There was no reply. He rubbed his stomach, the burning pain returning like an unwelcome guest at a party. How in hell did she manage to reduce him to the point where he responded like a child, throwing insults and barbs like some kid hurling clods of dirt.

Staring at the broken window, he thought of those moments before the brick had sailed through. He'd been about to make love to her. Even now, the memory of her fire-kissed near nakedness caused an immediate physical response. Damn her. And what was with that question about her sister?

Shaking his head, he went into the kitchen and grabbed a broom and a dustpan. There was no reason to leave the mess. The police would find no clues amid the broken glass.

After cleaning up the floor, he would need to find some sort of plywood to nail over the window until morning when somebody could come to fix it.

As he worked, he tried to make sense of his perverse attraction to Samantha. Despite his reluctance, he had to admit he felt a strong physical attraction to her. And her immediate response to him told him she felt the same crazy emotions where he was concerned. Irrationally, illogically, despite the fact he disliked so many things about her, he wanted her.

Better to recognize it, acknowledge it than to pretend it didn't exist, he thought, as he cleaned up the last of the glass. It took him a few minutes of rummaging in the shed to find a piece of plywood that would cover the broken window. He used more force than necessary to hammer in the nails, hoping the physical exertion would ease some of his lingering sexual ache.

If he were smart, he would leave here tonight, take up residence in a motel room somewhere until he could find another place to live. There was only one reason he wouldn't…couldn't do that.

He put the hammer down and picked up the brick and stared at the message. It seemed he wasn't the only person in town stirred up by Samantha.

The message was a warning and for the first time Tyler had to consider that Samantha might be right, that Dominic might be innocent. And if Dominic was innocent, that meant the real killer might have Samantha in his sights.

No, there was no way he could move out, leaving Samantha here alone with only a housekeeper who went home every night after dinner.

A heavy knock pounded on the door, followed by a deep voice announcing it was the police. As Tyler went to answer, he rubbed his stomach absently, knowing somehow that the inner peace he'd worked so hard to attain was about to be shattered. The orderly, upright life he'd made for himself was about to explode. All because of a murder case…and a leggy blonde named Samantha.

Chapter 7

"Thank you for seeing me, Mrs. Morgan," Samantha said to the gray-haired woman she'd seen briefly at Abigail Monroe's funeral.

"Oh, please, call me Georgia." She opened her front door wider to allow Samantha entry into the fashionable apartment. "Although I have to tell you, I'm confused as to why you want to talk to me." Her blue eyes radiated her bewilderment. "If you don't mind, we can talk in the kitchen. I'm in the middle of my bread making."

Samantha followed her through the tastefully decorated living room into a cheerful kitchen where the scent of warm dough and yeast greeted them. Georgia motioned Samantha into a chair at the table as she moved in front of the island, where a flour-covered cloth and a mountain of dough rested on the surface.

"I really appreciate you working me into your busy

schedule,'' Samantha said as Georgia dusted her hands with flour, then began to knead the dough.

Georgia Monroe was an attractive older woman. Although her hair was a steel gray, her features were youthful, her face curiously devoid of any deep wrinkles. Cosmetic surgery, Samantha suspected.

''Oh, dear, my schedule isn't like what it once was. When I was married to Morgan, my life was a nightmare of business dinners and hostess duties.'' Her hands worked the bread dough with dexterity. ''Now, my life is much less complicated, and more fulfilling.''

''How long were you married to Morgan?''

''Forty-two years. I married him when I was just nineteen.''

''And how long have you been divorced?'' Samantha asked as she pulled a small notepad from her pocket.

''It will be two years next month.''

''And was the divorce at your request or your husband's?''

Georgia quit working the dough and smiled ruefully. ''I was sixty-one years old at the time of our divorce. Hardly eager to join the ranks of the single set.'' She sighed. ''At that time, Morgan seemed to be going through some sort of midlife crisis. He started working out at the club, bought a flashy sports car and came home less and less. You might say he became a cliché, a man suddenly seeking his youth and thinking he'd found it in the arms of a young, beautiful blonde.''

''That must have hurt you deeply,'' Samantha said sympathetically. She paused for a moment, then added, ''You must have hated Abigail.''

Georgia smiled. ''Did you know Abigail?'' Samantha shook her head. ''It was impossible to hate her. She was so full of life and so beautiful it almost hurt to look at her. Initially I wanted to hate her, but I realized if it hadn't been Abigail, it would have been somebody else. Morgan wasn't happy with me, and I saw how happy Abigail made him. How could I hate her when she brought him such happiness?''

Although her words rang true, and Samantha saw no signs of tension or stress that would indicate lying, it seemed odd to Samantha that the first Mrs. Morgan would so embrace the younger, new Mrs. Morgan. But Samantha knew human emotions were nothing if not complex and strange.

Georgia seemed to sense Samantha's doubts. ''Look, Ms. Dark, I'm not going to pretend that I wasn't devastated when Morgan wanted a divorce. I love Morgan.'' She shook her head ruefully. ''I'll probably always love Morgan. But I've adjusted to my new life-style. I have my baking and my bridge club. My son lives here with me, and for the most part my life is rich and satisfying.''

She looked Samantha directly in the eye. ''If you think perhaps I had something to do with that poor girl's death, you're sadly mistaken.''

''I'm just gathering as much information as I can,'' Samantha told her. ''I believe Dominic Marcola is innocent and the best way to defend him against the charges is to make sure I have all the facts of the case before me.''

''Of course.'' Georgia nodded her head and began to knead the dough once again. ''But Dominic was found with her body and from what I've heard, had been drinking quite heavily. I'm just not sure what sort of information I can give you that will help you or his case.''

Samantha smiled. ''I think in that regard we're both

working in the dark." She flipped several pages in her notebook. "Your son's name is...?"

"Kyle." Georgia's eyes widened in horror. "Surely you don't think he had anything to do with the murder?"

"I'm just making sure I have my facts," Samantha replied. "And how old is Kyle?"

"He just turned twenty-one." Her strong features seemed to soften at thoughts of her son.

Samantha did a swift mental calculation. "You were forty-two when you had him?"

"A gift from heaven, that's what he was. My special angel from heaven."

At the moment, with her face shining with maternal love, it was impossible for Samantha to imagine this woman with her hands wrapped around Abigail Monroe's neck...impossible to imagine she was in any way involved in the murder. A wave of despair swept through Samantha.

"Can you think of any reason why anyone would want to murder Abigail?" she asked.

Georgia shook her head. "Oh, Abigail could be incredibly self-absorbed, at times downright selfish. But I can't imagine her making somebody so angry they'd want to...to kill her." Tears sparkled in Georgia's blue eyes. "Poor Abigail. And poor Morgan. He's utterly destroyed."

The sound of the front door opening halted Samantha's next question. "Mom, I'm home." Kyle Monroe's voice came from the living room.

"In the kitchen, dear."

Kyle entered the kitchen, the expectant smile on his face falling as he eyed Samantha. "What in the hell are you doing here?"

"Kyle, honey, Ms. Dark is just asking some questions." She flashed a quick smile at Samantha. "He's very protective of me." She wiped her hands on a towel and motioned Kyle into the chair opposite Samantha. "Sit down, Kyle. I'll make us all a nice cup of hot cocoa."

A handsome young man, Kyle Monroe had attitude to counter his attractiveness. "So, what do you want?" he asked Samantha, his dark eyebrows pulled together in a frown.

"I'd like to ask you a few questions," Samantha said, refusing to be daunted by Kyle's grim demeanor.

"No, I didn't like Abigail and no, I didn't kill her." Kyle's dark eyes radiated animosity.

"So you weren't happy when your father married her?"

"That's an understatement. My father was obviously thinking with other parts of his anatomy than his brain."

"Kyle!" Georgia sounded shocked.

The young man flushed. "It's true, Mom, and you know it. Abigail was nothing but a gold digger, and Dad was too stupid to see it."

Georgia's eyes flashed fire at her "gift from heaven." "That's enough, Kyle. I won't have you talking about your father that way." A steely strength underscored Georgia's words.

Kyle shoved away from the table, his face a thundercloud of emotion. Before his mother could stop him, he stormed out of the kitchen. A second later the front door slammed shut, signaling he'd left the house.

Georgia turned to Samantha, her features sagging. Suddenly she looked every one of her sixty-three years. "Please, don't think badly of Kyle. This whole ordeal has upset him tremendously. Morgan and I tried to keep him sheltered, perhaps too much so. With the divorce, then the murder, he's realizing the world isn't always a very nice place.''

Samantha nodded and stood. ''One more thing, and I'll get out of your hair. When was the last time you saw Abigail?''

Georgia frowned. ''I guess it was about three, four days before she was killed. We ran into each other downtown and shared lunch at the club.'' Once again, sparkling tears appeared in Georgia's faded blue eyes. ''She was so excited. She thought she might be pregnant, but I guess she wasn't because I never heard anything more about that…you know…after.''

Samantha tried to hide her surprise. She'd given the autopsy report a cursory read, but hadn't studied it in any depth. Now she couldn't wait to get back to her office and look at it once again. ''Thank you for your time. I appreciate you speaking so freely to me.''

Georgia took Samantha's hand in hers. ''If that young man you're representing isn't responsible for Abigail's murder, then I hope you find whoever is.'' She smiled, once again looking younger than her years. ''You like homemade cinnamon raisin bread?'' she asked suddenly as she dropped Samantha's hand.

''Sure,'' Samantha replied, disconcerted by the swift change of topic.

Georgia walked over to the cabinet by the oven, where several aluminum-foil-wrapped loaves sat in a row. Different colored ribbons belted each one. ''Cinnamon-raisin bread is my specialty. I bake it three times a week and give it to friends and family.'' She grabbed one with a red ribbon and handed it to Samantha. ''Red is for Tuesday. That means I baked this yesterday. Had you come a little later today you would have gotten one with a blue ribbon. Blue for Wednesday.''

Samantha walked to the front door, clutching the loaf of bread and fighting off a wave of sympathy for a woman who had so little in her life she color-coded her baked goods.

As she drove back to the office, her head whirled with suppositions. Had Abigail been pregnant? Had Samantha somehow missed that in the autopsy report? If there had been a pregnancy, was it possible that might have been a motive for her murder? But why?

At the office she was greeted by an empty receptionist's desk. She looked at her watch, surprised to discover it was after five. Where had the day gone? Where had the past week gone?

She went directly into her office and pawed through the piles of papers on her desk until she uncovered the autopsy report. Kicking off her shoes, she sank down on the overstuffed love seat across the room from the desk and began to read.

Tyler parked his car in the office parking lot, unsurprised to see Samantha's car still there despite the lateness of the hour.

He'd scarcely seen her in the past few days—since the night they'd nearly made love. He turned off his engine, allowing himself the memory of how she'd felt in his arms, how her body had looked with the kiss of firelight upon it.

Thank God. Thank God that brick had flown through the window, shattering whatever madness had gripped them both. And it had been a kind of madness. There was no other way to explain the firestorm of passion that had swept sanity away.

He got out of the car and used his key to enter the building. He needed to get some files from his office before heading home for the night. He noticed the light shining from beneath Jamison's office door. Samantha's office, he mentally amended.

Taking the stairs two at a time, he tried not to think of the woman in the other office, and instead focused on the one with whom he'd just shared dinner.

Thirty years old, Sarah Baylor was just the kind of woman Tyler had envisioned himself eventually marrying. Quietly pretty, with an eagerness to please, she'd made it clear she was definitely interested in more than just the occasional dinner date. A fourth-grade teacher with conservative views, Tyler knew Sarah would never do anything to embarrass him, or compromise his personal or professional integrity.

A month ago Tyler had seriously been entertaining thoughts of proposing to her. Tonight the idea seemed less than appealing.

He gathered up the files he'd wanted, then went back down the stairs. Starting out the door, he hesitated and looked back at Samantha's office door. She'd been keeping killer hours for the past week. Up and out before he awoke, and returning to the house long after he'd gone to bed. If she kept it up, she wouldn't be defending anyone. She would be in the hospital with a severe case of exhaustion.

He remembered the rush that had accompanied his first big case, knew Samantha was probably functioning on adrenaline alone. He also knew it wasn't healthy.

She had nobody else to tell her these things. Had Jamison been alive, he would have wanted Tyler to impress on her the importance of not burning herself out in the initial stages of a case.

Decision made, Tyler knocked softly on Samantha's office door. No reply. He knocked once again. When there was still no answer, he pushed open the door and stepped inside.

The lamp on her desk created a small pool of illumination, the glow carrying just far enough for him to see her curled up on the love seat.

Most of her hair had long ago escaped from the barrette at the nape of her neck and now cascaded around her head like a curtain of pale silk. One hand still clutched an array of papers while the other curled beneath her chin. She looked comfortable, at peace despite the contortion of her long legs in the small space.

He hesitated, wondering if he should waken her or just allow her to sleep through the night. He decided if he left her alone, she would probably not be able to use her legs in the morning.

"Samantha?" he called softly. She didn't move and he took a step closer. He could smell her now, the exotic fragrance of wildflowers and spice. He clenched his hands into fists at his sides, fighting the impulse to touch her, caress the soft skin of her cheek, run his fingers through the richness of her hair.

What would happen if he leaned down and touched his lips to hers? He frowned, irritated by his fanciful thoughts. Who the hell did he think he was? Prince Charming? No kiss from him was going to turn Samantha into a sweet, innocent princess.

"Samantha, wake up." He touched her shoulder, then jumped back. She gained consciousness with flailing fists and thrashing legs, and the papers she'd been holding fell to the floor.

As sleep dissipated, her eyes cleared and she sat up with a small moan. "What time is it?" she asked.

"A few minutes after nine."

"Dammit, that means I've been out for a couple of hours." She leaned over and gathered up the papers from the floor at her feet.

"Samantha." He placed a hand on her shoulder. "Why don't you give it a rest for the night?"

"I don't have time to give it a rest." She finished straightening the papers, then stood and walked over to her desk. "The trial is only a week away. There's still so much to be done."

Tyler heard the edge of panic in her voice, wondered if she was aware it was there. She sank down behind the desk and hunched her shoulders up and down, as if in an attempt to dispel tension.

Tyler sat on the edge of he desk, studying her features beneath the full glow of the desk lamp. "Why don't you ask for a continuance? You know Judge Halloran would probably give you more time to prepare for trial."

She shook her head. "Dominic refuses. He has the right to a speedy trial and that's what he's insisting on—although I've told him that with more time, perhaps more evidence could be uncovered—things that would point to his innocence."

She frowned and rubbed the center of her forehead with an index finger. "Unfortunately, Dominic seems to believe that I'm going to be able to pull a rabbit out of the hat. He has complete confidence in my ability to get him off and doesn't want to spend a day more than necessary in jail."

Tyler placed his fingers beneath her chin, forcing her to look up at him. "You won't be any good to him if you work yourself to death before this thing gets to trial. You've been pushing yourself too hard. You have dark circles under your eyes, and you've lost weight. You look like hell. When was the last time you had a decent meal?''

She jerked her chin away from his grasp. "If you came in here to make me feel better, you're not doing a very good job. And I had breakfast this morning."

"What? A doughnut at your desk?" The look on her face confirmed that he was right. He grabbed her by the arm and pulled her up out of the desk chair.

"Hey…what are you doing?" she sputtered in surprise as he propelled her across the floor toward the door. She struggled to get away from his firm grip.

He stopped at the door and turned to face her. "Samantha, the brain needs fuel, and fuel comes in the form of food." He didn't release his hold on her arm despite the mutinous expression on her face. "I'm taking you down to the Royale Restaurant where the dinner special tonight is a thick prime rib."

All signs of mutiny faded. "Prime rib with horseradish?"

He nodded. "Hot enough to blow smoke from your ears." He smiled softly, again noting how tired, how utterly dispirited she looked. "Come on, let your partner buy you some dinner. You can tell me what you've got on the Marcola case. Maybe a little brainstorming is in order."

"Really? You mean it?" She searched his face, as if suspecting a trick. "You wouldn't mind talking about the case?"

Tyler hesitated. The last thing he wanted to do was get involved in the Marcola case. From the little he'd heard about the case, there were too many similarities that reminded Tyler of the tragedy in his own life. He didn't want to relive memories he'd buried long ago.

Still, Samantha's face shone with hope as she looked up at him. He remembered those nights when he and Jamison had discussed aspects of their cases, sharing ideas, brainstorming strategy. Those times together had created mutual respect, an unbreakable bond between the two that future discord or arguments couldn't break. Suddenly Tyler wanted that with Samantha.

"Come on, we'll talk while you eat."

She smiled—a full, gorgeous smile that created a warming heat deep inside Tyler. Ignoring it, pretending it didn't even exist, he escorted her out of the building and to his car.

It took only moments to drive to the Royale Restaurant, Wilford's idea of upscale public dining. The hostess who greeted them as they entered raised an eyebrow at Tyler. "Busy night?" she said with a secretive smile as she led the two to a table in a private little alcove. Tyler felt himself blush, knowing the hostess referred to his date an hour earlier with Sarah.

Samantha eyed him curiously as she sat at the table and the hostess moved away. " 'Busy night'?"

"I was here a little earlier and had dinner."

"Alone?" She held up her hand before he could answer. "Sorry, that's really none of my business."

"Actually, I had a date," he replied, wondering why he felt like a philandering husband at the admission.

One of her pale eyebrows arched upward. "Anyone I know?"

"Sarah Baylor. She teaches fourth grade."

"Petite...blond?"

Tyler nodded in surprise. "You know her?"

Samantha shook her head. "No, but I think I saw you talking to her at Abigail's funeral."

"Yes, she was there." Tyler took a sip of his water.

"So tell me where you are in your investigation of the Marcola case," he said as he put his glass back down. For some reason it made him uncomfortable to discuss Sarah with Samantha.

She leaned forward, her eyes shining like rich toffee candies. "I've assigned Wylie to doing a little background on Abigail to find out if there's anything in her past that might have to do with her murder. By the way, thanks for talking him into helping me."

"Has he turned up anything useful?"

The sparkle in her eyes dimmed slightly. "Not yet."

"He's good, Samantha. If there's something to find, Wylie will dig it up."

Their conversation halted as a waitress arrived at the table. Samantha ordered the prime-rib dinner, Tyler wanted only coffee.

"I interviewed Georgia and Kyle Morgan today," Samantha said when the waitress had departed.

"And?"

"And I'm not sure." She frowned. As she unfolded her napkin in her lap, a wrinkle furrowed her brow. "Georgia was pleasant and that's more than I can say for Kyle. That kid seems to have an attitude problem."

Tyler tried to hide a smile. Of all people, it seemed ironic for Samantha to talk about a kid needing an attitude adjustment.

"Don't you dare say a word," Samantha warned, eyes narrowed as if she'd read his mind.

He laughed and held up his hands in supplication. "Not me. I wouldn't dare."

"Anyway," she continued, a spark of humor lighting her eyes, "he's not exactly in the running with me for Mr. Personality." The humor faded. "He hated Abigail, thought she was a gold digger after his father's money."

"You think maybe he had something to do with Abigail's death?"

"I don't know. Maybe. I'm going to have Wylie check him out. But, I discovered some interesting information from Georgia. Apparently she had lunch with Abigail a few days before the murder and Abigail told her she thought she was pregnant."

"Did you check the autopsy report?"

She nodded, her hair shining in the glow from the candle that lit the center of their table. "That's what I was doing when I fell asleep. According to the autopsy, she wasn't pregnant."

"So I guess that's a dead end," Tyler replied, wondering how it was that the candlelight did such magnificent things to her—things he hadn't noticed it doing to Sarah.

"I don't think so," she countered. "It doesn't matter so much whether or not she was actually pregnant. What matters is if she thought she was and who she might have told."

Tyler looked at her in surprise. The astuteness of her mind amazed him and he wasn't sure why. Perhaps it was because she'd always exhibited such a lack of judgment while growing up.

Once again their conversation came to a halt as the waitress arrived with Samantha's prime rib. For a few minutes talk was impossible as Samantha focused on the pleasure of filling her stomach.

She ate as she did everything—with gusto. Tyler leaned back in his chair and sipped his coffee, watching as she devoured the meal.

She seemed not to spare a thought for calories or cholesterol as she smothered her potato in sour cream and lathered the bread with butter.

He wondered if she made love with the same wild abandon. Somehow he imagined so. There would be no worry about messing her hair, no fear of unflattering positions. She would throw herself into the act as she did everything in her life—intensely and passionately.

"I'm sorry...I didn't realize how famished I was," she said, her words of apology making Tyler realize he'd been frowning at her. She wiped her mouth with the napkin. "Now, where were we...? Oh, yes. Abigail's pregnancy."

As Samantha told Tyler her thoughts, he tried to focus on her words, on the case—and forget the mental images of Samantha and lovemaking. "Dominic said Abigail was excited, almost high with a secret that she said assured her a wonderful settlement from Morgan. Could the secret be that she thought she was pregnant?"

Samantha frowned. "That would be my initial thought, but I'm not sure exactly how she thought a baby would garner her a fortune. Sure, Morgan would have to pay child support, but that would be all she could expect. No, I think there's got to be something more to Abigail's secret than the prospect of motherhood. I also think finding out what her secret was might give us a solid clue as to who killed her."

"So what kind of defense are you building in case you don't discover the real perpetrator?" Tyler asked.

The waitress appeared to refill Tyler's coffee cup and take away Samantha's empty plate. Samantha ordered a piece of pie and coffee, then when the waitress had once again left, she leaned back in her chair, a troubled expression on her face. "The only things I've really got are some sloppy police work, some inconsistent factors, and the hope that the jury will see how ridiculous the whole prosecution case against Dominic really is."

"Let me play devil's advocate here," he suggested.

She nodded and leaned forward. Again he noticed the shine in her eyes—the shine of intelligence, emotion and belief. If the jury could look into her eyes, they would believe whatever she had to say, he thought.

"First, there're the toxicology reports. Both Abigail's and Dominic's blood showed a high concentration of barbiturates, and the alcohol level in them both was well below the legal definition of inebriation. Odd, isn't it?"

Tyler nodded. What he found even more odd was the fact that he had so much trouble concentrating on her words. Odd to realize that although he'd known her for years, he really didn't know her at all. He'd never before noticed that her hair wasn't just a single shade of blond, but rather a hundred different shades of "pretty." He'd never noticed before that her smile always began first in her eyes, lighting up their darkness before curving her lips.

"What's even more odd is that nobody tested the champagne. The bottle was accidentally thrown out."

Her words penetrated his mind. "You think it might have been drugged?"

"It's the only thing that makes sense. Dominic said he didn't drink enough to be drunk, but he felt woozy and then passed out. He said the bottle was already open when he arrived, that about half of it was gone when he and Abigail started drinking it."

Her words garnered Tyler's full attention. "Go on," he said thoughtfully.

"In my interview with Morgan, I asked him about Abigail's drinking habits. He said she always had several glasses of champagne in the evenings. She loved the stuff and always had a bottle in the refrigerator. That, coupled with the 911 call that came from two blocks away from the murder scene, certainly creates reasonable doubt in my mind as to exactly what happened that night.''

"The whole case would be much stronger if you could hint at other people with motives for murder," he observed.

"No problem." She flashed him one of her quicksilver smiles. "I can begin with Kyle Monroe, who might have heard that Abigail thought she was pregnant and was afraid of what a new baby and wife would do to his inheritance. Then there's Morgan himself, who despite his alibi could have hired a killer to get rid of the new wife who'd married him only for his money. And I have a feeling when Wylie finishes investigating Abigail's background, he'll have a host of other suspects for me to use in Dominic's defense. And I'm still hopeful that if this was a hired killing, by keeping his ear to the floor, Bones will hear something useful."

"You never did tell me how you met Bones," Tyler said.

"Bones was one of the cohorts I ran with when I was in high school. He helped me sneak out of the house on more than one occasion."

Tyler's stomach muscles knotted as he wondered if Bones had been one of her boyfriends. Had he been an intimate partner in Samantha's rebellions against her father? He was surprised and disturbed to discover that it was jealousy that clenched his stomach. Irritation usurped the unwanted emotion. Rather than focusing it inward, he vented it on her. "You broke your father's heart with those teenage rebellions."

The warmth in her eyes dissipated, turning frosty in a split second. "He broke my heart time and time again. You weren't around in those first years after my mother died. You didn't see the way Father chipped away at me. You saw only the great Jamison Dark, the charismatic orator and legal eagle. You didn't see the man—the father figure so cold and distant, the man who told me over and over again that I was nothing and never would be anything.''

Tyler studied her features and saw the tension, the pain that radiated from her whenever she spoke of her dad. "Samantha, is that what this case is about? Did you take it to prove yourself to your father? He's dead, Samantha. You can't prove anything to him."

She smiled, a sad gesture that didn't reach the shadows in her eyes. "You really don't get it, do you, Tyler? This isn't about proving anything to my father. This is about proving something to myself. If I win, then I'll know I'm worthwhile and I can do good things.... If I lose, I'll know my father was right all along. I'll know that I'm nothing—that I'll never be anything more than nothing."

"Samantha, this is just a case," Tyler protested.

"No, Tyler. This is just my life." She started as the waitress appeared at their table and placed her chocolate pie in front of her.

She ate silently, her gaze focused on the candle flame. Tyler knew he was about to do something incredibly stupid. He fought against it, but knew it was to no avail. The stakes of the Marcola case had just risen, and suddenly it was important to him that she win. "Samantha, I know I said I didn't want anything to do with this case, but if you want me to, I'd be glad to second chair you."

His reward was the warmth returning to her eyes and a beatific smile covering her face. "There are times when you show definite signs of promise, Sinclair,'' she said softly.

Tyler sighed, wondering if in trying to help Samantha save her soul, he might not lose his own.

Chapter 8

Tyler came awake gasping for air, his heart in his throat as he waited for the nightmare to loosen its grasp on him. He sat up on the edge of the bed, his heart still thundering.

He'd thought he'd finally outgrown the nightmares. But for the past week, since agreeing to help Samantha on the Marcola case, they had been an unwanted nightly visitor.

The light of dawn crept in through his windows. It filled the room with a surreal golden glow that brought him a modicum of relief, like that of a child awakening from a bad dream and seeing the reassuring illumination from a night-light.

He raked a hand through his hair and stood in an attempt to cast the last of the nightmare images out of his mind.

Padding over to the window, he wondered how Samantha had slept. Dominic's trial began today, and he and Samantha had been up until late the night before, going over last-minute details.

A jury of eight women and four men would ultimately decide the fate of Dominic Marcola. Samantha had been pleased by the female-dominated selection of jurists, insisting that women would believe a man who loved the victim incapable of such a heinous crime.

Tyler, as usual playing devil's advocate, had reminded her that many of the people who killed professed to love their victims.

A lively argument had followed, Samantha maintaining that real love couldn't kill, and Tyler certain that it could. As the debate had continued, Samantha's intensely romantic viewpoint surprised him, provoking his own latent cynicism. She made him realize that he'd long ago discarded the notion of true and lasting love.

Turning away from the window, Tyler headed for the shower. As he stood beneath hot needles of water, the last of his nightmare was banished, washed down the drain with any remaining sleepiness. He had a feeling that it was going to be a long day.

Moments later, clad in one of his power business suits, he headed downstairs, where the scent of fresh brewed coffee greeted him. Looking at his watch, he realized it was too early for Virginia. He walked into the kitchen and saw Samantha sitting at the table, a cup of coffee in front of her.

"All ready for your big day?"

"Piece of cake," she replied with an overbright smile, although he saw her hand tremble slightly as she raised her cup to her mouth.

He poured himself some coffee, then joined her at the table. "You hungry? I could whip us up a little breakfast," he said. "Maybe some eggs, sunny-side up, with a slab of ham on the side?"

She turned a little green around the gills. "No, thanks. I work best with an edge of hunger gnawing at me."

He nodded, amused that she obviously didn't want him to know just how nervous she was. He remembered well the feeling of his first official day in court—the rush of adrenaline swooping through him, coupled with a dizzying need to throw up. Welcome to the big league, he thought, but quickly assured her, "You'll do fine."

"I intend to do better than fine," she snapped. "I'm planning on something approaching greatness."

He grinned at her forced bravado. If her willpower counted at all, he had no doubt she would approach something close to greatness. Had she not been so nervous, he would have been worried about her performance in court. Had she not had the look of a deer caught in the glare of an approaching car's headlights, he would have doubted her capacity. Yes, she would do fine.

"Excuse me," she said and shoved away from the table. She bolted out of her chair and disappeared down the hallway. He heard the slam of the bathroom door and grinned. Yes, she would be just fine—as soon as she finished throwing up.

A few minutes before eight o'clock, Tyler and Samantha got into his car to drive to the courthouse. Court would begin at nine, and Samantha wanted time to talk to Dominic before the trial began.

As Tyler drove, he shot surreptitious looks at his partner.

She looked exceedingly attractive in a conservative skirt and jacket she'd bought specifically for the occasion. The dark brown emphasized her hair, which was braided into a neat length down her back, and brought out the rich darkness of her eyes, which sparkled in anticipation of a good fight.

She was talking softly to herself, and Tyler heard enough to know she was going over her opening statement. She fell silent as they pulled into a parking space across from the county courthouse and she saw the chaos taking place on the steps of the building.

"That snake," she muttered as she spied Chester Sparks speaking before a live videocam. "The trial hasn't even officially begun yet and he's trying to sway public opinion."

"Samantha..." Tyler warned as he saw the light of battle in her eyes. "Don't do anything crazy."

She grabbed her briefcase and grinned at him as they got out of the car. "Don't worry. I told you I thought my picture would look terrific splashed across the front pages of the paper." She flashed him another smile that set his ulcer to work. "We're going to see just how good I look," she said and started walking toward the camera.

Tyler watched as the media people noticed her, knew that interviewing the defense counsel in a murder case was much more appealing than talking to the prosecution, especially when the defense counsel was a good-looking blonde with shapely legs.

To Tyler's surprise, Samantha handled the reporters as if she'd been doing it for years. Using humor and quick wit, she managed to convey utter confidence in her client and his innocence without giving away any specifics of their case.

"Hey, Tyler."

He turned to see Gary Watters, a reporter for the Wilford paper, approaching him. "No comment, Gary."

Gary grinned. "I haven't asked you anything yet." He moved closer to Tyler and held out a tape recorder. "Come on, just answer a few questions. You don't want me to lose my job, do you?"

Tyler laughed good-naturedly. "Gary, we both know you're Wilford's answer to Jimmy Olson. Your job certainly isn't dependent on my answering your questions."

"Just tell me why you aren't heading this defense."

"Because my partner is," Tyler answered easily.

"Is she as good as her father was?"

"Better."

"There are rumors that there's more than business going on between you and the attractive Ms. Dark."

"That's ridiculous," Tyler scoffed, then winced in irritation. "No more questions," he said and shouldered his way past the reporter.

With questions still pelting them, Samantha and Tyler made their way into the relative quiet of the building. Samantha vibrated with energy, her cheeks flushed with excitement. As they went into the conference room that had been provided them to meet with their client, she turned to him. "Tell me I can do this, Tyler." Her hand trembled with need as she grabbed his. "Tell me you believe in me."

As always, seeing the vulnerable side of Samantha disconcerted him. Knowing that his opinion of her was important touched him in a secret place that hadn't been touched in a very long time.

He framed her face with his hands, saw the self-doubts that suddenly darkened her eyes, knew the unexpected fear that caused her pulse to flutter in the hollow of her throat. "Samantha, I've never believed in anyone like I believe in you at this moment." A responding warmth seemed to shoot directly from her eyes into his heart. "Your father would have been so proud of you," he added.

Her eyes narrowed and she stepped away from him. "Don't ruin my day by bringing him into the conversation."

She walked over to the table and placed her briefcase on top.

Tyler watched as she pulled her papers from the case, her movements jerky with suppressed anger. "Samantha, sooner or later you're going to have to deal with your feelings about your dad. Sooner or later you're going to have to forgive him. For your own sake."

Her eyes flashed fire as she looked at him. "Right now, all I have to do for my sake is win this case. I don't owe my father forgiveness. I don't owe him anything."

The conversation halted as an officer opened the door to admit Dominic. Immediately they focused on preparing Dominic for his days in court.

At precisely nine o'clock, the case of the *State of Missouri* v. *Marcola* began. Chester Sparks, clad in a beige suit with a bright salmon-colored tie, delivered his opening statement in his usual fire-and-brimstone style. Raising his voice like a minister casting out demons, he spewed saliva, his face red with exertion as he boomed to the jury. The jurists visibly shrank back in their chairs—whether dodging spittle or simply wanting distance, Tyler wasn't sure.

As Samantha stood to begin her statement, Tyler's stomach clenched with spasms of nervous tension. Samantha's style was conversational, friendly. She eyed each of the jurists, smiling confidently, as if secretly telling them she knew they were brilliant and would agree with her assessment of the case.

Tyler began to relax as he watched the jury members respond to her. They leaned forward, listening intently as she calmly laid out how she intended to prove Dominic wouldn't, couldn't and hadn't killed Abigail Monroe.

As she finished and walked back to her place at the defense table, she passed Chester. She whispered something to him and his face paled, then reddened. For a moment he seemed completely disoriented.

"Mr. Sparks? Your first witness?" the judge prompted.

"Yes, of course…" He thumbed through his paperwork and cleared his throat a number of times, his face reddening once again as he cast a furtive glance at Samantha.

Tyler leaned over to his partner. "You broke his concentration, destroyed his rhythm. What on earth did you say to him?" he whispered.

She grinned, her brown eyes sparkling mischievously. "I told him my underpanties were the same color as his tie."

Tyler wasn't sure whether to be appalled or amused. It was just the sort of improper behavior he didn't approve of, and yet he couldn't argue with the results. As a battle tactic, it was brilliant. Chester Sparks was still trying to regain his composure. Tyler leaned back toward Samantha. "You're something else," he whispered in her ear.

She flashed him a smile. "I'm only just beginning."

"Tell me again…I was good, wasn't I?" Samantha asked when they entered the house at the end of the long day. Filled with energy, she walked into the study where Virginia had left a fire burning. She flipped on the stereo, wanting music. She felt like singing, like dancing, like shouting out loud.

Tyler leaned against the doorjamb, an amused smile on his face as she kicked off her high heels and dug her toes into the thick carpeting. "You were good," he agreed. "It went very well, but you've got to remember, this is just the first day," he warned her. "It's going to be a long trial. You'll have good moments and there will be bad moments."

Samantha shook her head as if to discount his warning. She didn't want to hear anything negative. She wanted to celebrate. "Admit it, I kicked butt," she said.

Tyler laughed. "You kicked butt."

She nodded. "You hungry? I'm famished. Let's go see what Virginia left us for dinner."

Minutes later they sat at the table eating roast-beef sandwiches and digesting the events of the day. "I couldn't believe it when Officer Winstead said he thought the 911 call was suspicious. It was like a gift from heaven falling in my lap," Samantha said as she reached for more potato chips.

"He's a rookie cop, too young to know you don't volunteer personal opinion like that. Somebody will chew him up for his lapse on the stand."

"And then the forensics guy admitted they'd made a mistake when they tossed the champagne bottle." Euphoria swept over Samantha as she remembered the look on the jurists' faces at this information. "If the jury had gone to deliberate tonight, I'd win."

"Unfortunately, they don't deliberate tonight and to-morrow Chester might have a good day."

Samantha frowned at him. "Why are you trying to rain on my parade?"

"I'm not," he protested. "I'm just trying to keep you firmly on the ground."

Samantha looked down at her plate, finding the warmth radiating from his eyes uncomfortably evocative, the gentle caring in his tone surprisingly welcome. She tried to focus on the conversation, not his physical appeal. "I know today is just the first day and I got lucky with a couple of the prosecution witnesses. I know tomorrow might be a very different tale. But for tonight, I just want to ride my high. Is that so horribly wrong?"

"No, it's not." He smiled. "I remember the very first day of my very first case. I, too, had a good day and felt giddy with power, wild with success. Your father told me I was still wet behind the ears and had too much to learn to waste time feeling good about myself."

Samantha nodded, remembering all the times her father had verbally kicked the confidence out of her. "He was good at deflating egos." She stood and put their dirty dishes in the dishwasher. She didn't want to think about her father. Tyler's words earlier in the day about forgiveness had bothered her. She knew he was right; sooner or later she was going to have to come to terms with her anger concerning her father. But not tonight. Tonight she wanted to fly on wings of celebration.

Although it was nearly ten o'clock and it had been a grueling day, she was too wired to go to bed. Tyler stood and stretched and as Samantha gazed at him, warmth spread through her.

He'd spent the entire day in court sitting next to her, supporting her not only emotionally, but in every other capacity as well. All day long she'd smelled his scent,

GET A FREE TEDDY BEAR...

You'll love this plush, cuddly Teddy Bear, an adorable accessory for your dressing table, bookcase or desk. Measuring 5½" tall, he's soft and brown and has a bright red ribbon around his neck – he's completely captivating! And he's yours *absolutely free*, when you accept this no-risk offer!

AND TWO FREE BOOKS!

Here's a chance to get **two free Silhouette Intimate Moments® novels** from the Silhouette Reader Service™ **absolutely free!**

There's no catch. You're under no obligation to buy anything. We charge nothing – ZERO – for your first shipment. And you don't have to make any minimum number of purchases – not even one!

Find out for yourself why thousands of readers enjoy receiving books by mail from the Silhouette Reader Service. They like the **convenience of home delivery**…they like getting the best new novels months before they're available in bookstores…and they love our **discount prices!**

Try us and see! Return this card promptly. We'll send your free books and a free Teddy Bear, under the terms explained on the back. We hope you'll want to remain with the reader service – but the choice is always yours! (U-SIL-IM- 04/98) **245 SDL CF4T**

NAME _____

ADDRESS _____ APT. _____

CITY _____ STATE _____ ZIP _____

Offer not valid to current Silhouette Intimate Moments® subscribers. All orders subject to approval.

©1993 HARLEQUIN ENTERPRISES LIMITED   Printed in U.S.A.

▲ CLAIM YOUR FREE BOOKS AND FREE GIFT! RETURN THIS CARD TODAY! ▲

NO OBLIGATION TO BUY!

If offer card is missing write to: Silhouette Reader Service, 3010 Walden Ave., P.O. Box 1867, Buffalo, NY 14240-1867

BUSINESS REPLY MAIL
FIRST-CLASS MAIL   PERMIT NO. 717   BUFFALO, NY

POSTAGE WILL BE PAID BY ADDRESSEE

SILHOUETTE READER SERVICE
3010 WALDEN AVE
PO BOX 1867
BUFFALO NY 14240-9952

NO POSTAGE
NECESSARY
IF MAILED
IN THE
UNITED STATES

felt his body heat beside her. When she scored a hit with her cross-examination, he'd grabbed her hand as she sat back down at the table, his eyes warming her with praise.

"Don't go to bed yet," she said, knowing that was probably his intention. She reached out and took his hand. "Let's have a celebration party."

"It's kind of late for guests."

"A party with just you and me." She tugged at his hand. "Come on. Come into the study and dance with me." She felt his hesitation. "Please, Tyler. This has been the best day of my life, and I'm not ready for it to end yet."

He smiled. "The lady wants to dance? Let's dance."

And they did. With the stereo blaring golden oldies and the fire blazing, they twisted and two-stepped, strolled and macarenaed. Samantha was surprised but pleased to discover that Tyler was a good dancer. He moved with a natural grace and rhythm. Before long they'd both shed their suit jackets. Tyler pulled off his tie and Samantha untucked her blouse.

While they danced, they discussed the high points of the day and plotted strategy for the following one. Samantha had never felt so alive. She didn't want the night to end. She wanted to bottle her happiness to keep forever.

When the radio station began a soft, mellow tune, she moved into Tyler's arms for their first slow dance. She didn't want to think about all the reasons why she shouldn't be in his arms—nebulous reasons that were so easy to forget as he held her close.

She coiled her arms up around his neck, able to feel his heart beating rapidly against her own. Suddenly she remembered the night when the brick had come flying through the window, the night she'd almost made love to him.

Oh, she'd wanted him on that night. His kiss had stirred the place deep inside her that had never been touched by a man; had called forth a response she'd never felt before.

She raised her head and looked at him, knowing she wanted that again. She wanted him to kiss her, sweep away all rational thought. She wanted to make love to him.

He must have seen her desire in her eyes, for she felt the catch of breath in his chest as he stared back at her. His arms tightened around her, his hands splaying across her back, then moving down to cup her buttocks. "Kiss me, Tyler," she said softly. "Kiss me, then make love to me. I want you so badly."

His mouth captured hers with fiery hunger. There was no pretense of dancing anymore. Although the music swirled around them, their feet stopped moving the moment the kiss began.

Samantha returned the kiss with a hunger of her own, tangling her tongue with his, an active participant in stoking the flames of passion. He pulled her closer against him and she felt his desire, bold and thrusting against her.

As the kiss came to an end, she leaned her head back, allowing his lips access to the length of her neck. Shivers of delight raced up her spine as he nibbled and licked and teased her skin.

While he loved her throat and ears, she worked the buttons on his dress shirt, wanting to see his chest, feel it naked beneath her fingertips. When she'd unfastened the last button, he shrugged out of the shirt, exposing his beautifully muscled chest dusted with dark, curling hairs.

She started to unbutton her own blouse, but paused as he caught her hands in his. "Let me," he whispered. Almost reverently, he unfastened each button, pausing to kiss each inch of skin he exposed.

As her blouse fell to the floor, Samantha's knees weakened and she sank down to the carpeting in front of the fire.

Tyler joined her, taking her in his arms as his fingers worked the hook at the back of her bra. When the wispy material joined her blouse on the floor, he sat back for a moment and simply looked at her, his eyes blazing with a flame to rival the fire. "You are so beautiful." His voice was low and husky.

He reached for her, pulling her beneath him as they stretched out full length. His chest warmed hers, his coarse chest hair providing erotic stimulation against her nipples. He kissed her again—a deep, soul-searing kiss that stole away her breath and any lingering doubts she might entertain.

With trembling fingers, she reached for the snap and zipper of his slacks. She knew if she touched him there, she would cross a line and there would be no going back for either of them. And that was what she wanted.

No doubts. No regrets. She felt as if she'd lived half her life just waiting for this moment to happen with Tyler. It had always been as inevitable as her next breath.

As her fingers moved to unzip his slacks, he moaned, a sound that elevated Samantha's desire to new heights. She was in uncharted territory now. She'd never known desire could cause such an ache, never before known this kind of longing for fulfillment.

He kicked off his slacks, leaving himself clad only in a pair of cotton briefs that did little to hide his bold need.

A niggling fear whispered through Samantha as she removed her skirt and pulled off her panty hose, leaving only a pair of lacy coral-colored panties. She knew she was about to give to Tyler a piece of herself she would never be able to retrieve. It scared her—and thrilled her. She reached for Tyler once again, wanting him to get on with it before she changed her mind, to possess her before her sanity returned.

He moved away from her slightly and propped his elbow up beneath him. "Slow," he said as his fingers danced across her collarbone, then stroked her breasts. "We're going to take this very slow." She shivered at the promise in his voice, at the heat of his gaze.

He dipped his head and captured one of her nipples between his lips, his tongue flicking at the turgid tip while his other hand slowly caressed the flatness of her abdomen.

Samantha felt as if she'd lost all control of her body and mind. She was nothing but a quivering mass of nerve endings. Each touch, each caress sent her higher.

When he finally touched the silk of her panties, she arched up to meet his hands, fear succumbing to need. Gently, he pulled the panties off her hips and down her legs, tossing them aside.

She'd always thought she would be embarrassed to be completely naked with a man. But Tyler didn't give her time to be embarrassed. When he touched her again, a sob caught in her throat—a sob of surprise and of splendor.

"You are so beautiful," he said, and then his mouth covered hers.

He stroked her until she thought she would lose her mind. Any control she had left snapped beneath the mastery of his caresses. He knew just where to touch, just where to kiss to take her to heights she'd never climbed before. Selflessly he plied her body with kisses and caresses until she reached the pinnacle and spun into the blackness of utter sensation.

When he started her on the same climb again, she stopped him, this time wanting him with her. She wanted him to lose control, lose himself in her. She reached down and touched the waistband of his briefs and in that instant, she knew his control had snapped.

With a frantic movement, he shed the last barrier that existed between them and moved on top of her. As he entered her, his eyes held hers, speaking in a language as old as time, showing his loss of control as wonderment stole across his features—wonderment that turned into confusion.

He stopped all movement, frozen in shock. "Samantha, you're—"

"Shh, don't say it, and don't stop." She wrapped her arms around the broadness of his back, trying to physically pull him closer, more tightly into her. Before he could make a move, she arced up to him. A dizzying stab of pain riveted through her. Tears sprang to her eyes as the pain subsided and pleasure swept through her. "It's okay," she whispered breathlessly. "Please…love me."

Tentatively he moved against her. "Yes…" she moaned. "Oh, yes." She watched as the surprise melted from his eyes, dissolving with each move of her hips against his. Then she closed her eyes and lost the last of herself.

It wasn't until he'd rolled off her and her breathing

had slowly returned to normal that she opened her eyes
and gazed at Tyler. Once again he was on his side, his
elbow propped beneath him as he gazed at her, his expression impossible to read.

"My, my, Mr. Sinclair. You do know how to throw
a celebratory party," she said lightly. She frowned
when he didn't respond in kind. "Tyler, please. Please,
don't say anything." She sat up and pushed her hair
away from her face. "Don't insult me by telling me
what a mistake we just made. It wasn't a mistake." She
eyed him defiantly. "I wanted to do it."

The waning firelight had cast his features in dark
shadow, making it impossible for her to guess what he
was thinking, what he was feeling.

"Why me?"

"Why not?" she countered flippantly. "I had a
whim, you were handy, and I didn't notice you pro-
testing too much." She stood and walked over to where
her panties had landed.

Aware of his gaze, she pulled them on. "You'll have
to excuse me, I don't know much about after-sex eti-
quette. Do we kiss now? Say good-night? Have a cig-
arette?" She spied a telltale muscle clenching in his
jaw. She knew she was being too glib and was making
him angry. But, what did he expect? That she whisper
how much she loved him? That she tell him she'd felt
the earth move and a piece of him crawl into her heart?

No way. She'd always known she wasn't the kind of
woman Tyler could love. He could desire her, want her
again and again, but she would never own his heart—
and she would never allow him to own hers. She'd
learned a long time ago that loving somebody gave that
person the power to hurt. Her father had taught her well;

she would never allow anyone to have that power over her again.

"I still don't understand," he said.

"What's to understand? Don't make this into something it's not. It's no big deal." They both jumped as the phone rang.

Tyler leaned over to pick up the receiver from the phone on the coffee table. As he answered, Samantha grabbed her blouse from the floor and pulled it on.

"It's for you," he said.

She took the receiver from him, wondering who would be calling at this time of night. "Hello?"

"Sam, got some news for you." Bones's deep voice whispered across the line.

"What?" She frowned, trying to shift mental gears.

"Word on the street is that there's a target on your head."

"Pardon me?" Samantha wondered if she'd heard him correctly. "Why?"

"Somebody wants you off the Marcola case real bad. And right now."

A chill raced up Samantha's spine. "Who?"

"Don't know. The only thing I do know is that whoever it is, they're offering five thousand big ones to put you out of commission. That's all I know."

"You'll tell me if you hear anything else?"

"You know it." Without saying goodbye, he clicked off.

Samantha replaced the receiver slowly, trying to digest what she'd just learned. She turned to Tyler, who'd pulled on his slacks and was buttoning his shirt. "That was Bones," she said. "He had some news for me." Tyler waited expectantly. "It seems somebody has put out a contract on me. Someone wants me dead."

Chapter 9

"Somebody wants me dead."

Samantha's words haunted Tyler for the remainder of the night and continued to worry him through the boring, forensic morning testimony.

After Bones's chilling phone call, Tyler and Samantha had talked, trying to figure out whose toes she might have stepped on, who the threat might have come from. But there were no answers.

Tyler was frightened for her. He sensed danger swirling closer and closer but felt a helpless impotence to stop it. Not only was he worried about her, he was worried about himself and the crazy confusion of his thoughts where she was concerned.

He stifled a yawn and sat up straighter at the defense table. At the moment, the hair and fiber expert was on the stand explaining every hair and fiber he'd found in Abigail Monroe's bedroom.

He cast Samantha a quick glance. She seemed completely oblivious to the turmoil she'd created in him. The testimony from the tall, thin hair-and-fiber expert captured her attention. She stopped looking at the man only long enough to make a quick note or two in the legal pad before her.

No big deal—that was what she'd insisted she felt about their lovemaking. No big deal. Tyler frowned and stared down at the table, once again overwhelmed with confusion.

For him it had been a very big deal. Making love to Samantha, discovering her a virgin, had shattered every preconceived notion he had about her.

Many nights he'd sat and listened to Jamison bemoan his eldest daughter's suspected promiscuity. The fact that Samantha had given herself completely and fully for the first time to Tyler, filled his heart with a burden he'd never felt before.

Why had she made love with him? He looked at her, noticing that as usual, tendrils of hair had escaped the neat confinement at the nape of her neck. She seemed to show no emotional baggage whatsoever from their lovemaking.

They'd been stiff and formal with each other over their morning coffee, neither mentioning what had happened the night before.

Tyler had recognized her diatribe immediately after their lovemaking as a defense mechanism. He also knew people were usually defensive because they were guilty or hiding something. What would Samantha be like without that edge of defensiveness, without the bravado that drove her from one mishap to another? He doubted he would ever know.

For the first time, Tyler wondered about the childhood she had said was so horrid, about what kind of father Jamison really had been to his two daughters. Had Samantha been right when she'd accused Tyler of being blinded by Jamison's charisma? Had Tyler seen only what he'd wanted to see in the man who had been his mentor?

He looked at Samantha once again, remembering how soft, how silky her skin had been beneath his touch, the way they'd fit together so perfectly as he'd slid deep inside her. A responding warmth spread through him even now, and he felt a stirring in his groin.

He jerked his gaze away from her, irritated that sheer memory alone could cause such a swift, potent reaction. Just what he needed—to have an obsessive desire for a woman with a penchant for trouble and a price on her head.

Tyler shifted his chair a little farther away from Samantha as the hair-and-fiber guy left the stand and the pathologist took his place. Maybe he could concentrate better on what was happening with the trial without the scent of Samantha fogging his brain, he thought.

The moment the first photograph of the victim was flashed on a screen, Tyler knew he was in trouble. He stared at the picture of the dead young woman and remembered another dead woman. His stomach churned and he felt a dizzying nausea sweep through him. Just like his nightmares. Haunting visions filled his head— visions he'd tried to forget since he was a fourteen-year-old kid.

Jerking his gaze from the picture, he drew in several deep breaths to steady himself. He closed his eyes and still the visions came. Fast and furious, they filled his mind.

He jumped as Samantha touched his arm, then leaned toward him. "You all right?" she whispered.

Her features swam before him as he fought against the soul sickness that gripped him. "Fine," he answered faintly. "I'll be fine."

He could tell by her expression that he hadn't convinced her.

When the judge called on her to cross-examine the pathologist, Samantha suggested they break for lunch. The judge agreed, and moments later Tyler and Samantha walked into a private conference room.

"Tell me," she said the moment she'd closed the door behind them. "What's going on?"

"Nothing. It's nothing." He paced the room, hoping he could walk off the haunting visions.

"Tyler, something got to you in there. Please, talk to me. Am I messing something up with the case?"

He turned to face her as she sank down at the conference table. Raking a hand through his hair, he wondered if telling somebody about that night would finally rid him of the nightmares, would finally exorcise the demons that haunted him. "Those pictures of Abigail...they reminded me of my mother."

"Your mother?" Samantha's voice was soft.

Turning toward the window, he focused his gaze outside, where treetops were visible from this third-story vantage point. As he watched, the trees seemed to melt and instead he was back on the streets in the St. Louis neighborhood where he'd grown up.

"I was fourteen and had been hanging out with my friends. My curfew came and went, but I didn't want to go home. I knew my mother's boyfriend was at the apartment, and I couldn't stand him. He was the last in a long line of losers she'd dated." His voice sounded cool, distant even to his own ears.

"All my friends started to head home, and so I did,

too. When I rounded the corner I saw police cars in front of our apartment building.'' He placed a hand on his stomach, where a thick dread churned. ''I think I knew then that she was dead...that he'd killed her.''

''Oh, Tyler, how awful.''

He heard the sound of Samantha rising, felt her presence just behind him, but he didn't turn to her. Caught up in the horror of his memory, he continued. ''The officers tried to stop me from going in, but somehow I got past them and ran up the six flights to our floor. A cop stood just outside and I dodged around him and into her bedroom.'' He drew a deep breath, feeling as if there wasn't enough oxygen in the room. ''She was on the bed. She looked like she was sleeping.''

He turned and looked at Samantha. ''For a minute I thought it was all a mistake, that she was going to wake up and everything would be fine. Then I saw that the front of her nightgown was covered in blood and I knew nothing would ever be fine again.''

''Tyler, I'm so sorry.'' She moved toward him and put her arms around his neck, warming him with her body heat as she hugged him tightly. He leaned his head against her shoulder, allowing her to comfort him as he had comforted her when she'd cried about her father.

''You should have told me about this sooner,'' she said as her hand stoked his hair. ''We could have seen to it that you weren't in court during the pathologist's testimony.''

He moved out of her arms, embarrassed by his show of weakness. ''It's okay. I'll be fine now. The picture of Abigail just shocked me, rocked me back in time.''

Samantha once again sat down at the table. ''You want to order in some lunch?'' she asked.

He shook his head. ''I'm not hungry.''

"Me neither."

He was aware of her gaze on him as he moved back to the window and once again looked outside. He'd hoped by telling Samantha about his mother, he would somehow free himself.

But the memories kept coming—the flashing police lights, the removal of her body from the apartment, the crying, pathetic apologies of her murderer as he stood handcuffed nearby. And with that memory came a crippling anger. He tried to push it away, knowing the destructiveness of such an emotion.

"This is why you don't do murder cases, isn't it?" Samantha's voice pulled him back from the brink of a dark pit.

He turned to look at her once again and nodded. "I never believed I could be objective enough to defend a murderer. I was always afraid my own emotions would get in the way of a good defense."

"What happened to your mother's killer?"

Exhausted from the emotional turmoil the conversation had wrought, Tyler sank into the chair across from her. "His name was Doug Woods. He plea-bargained. Got seven years." His bitterness bled into the tone of his voice.

"Why a defense lawyer? I would have thought with this kind of experience you would have become a prosecutor," she observed.

He smiled for the first time since entering the conference room. "For a while, my sole purpose in living was to get big enough, strong enough to kill Doug Woods when he got out of prison. Then I met your father. After a succession of foster homes, I was so hungry for adult attention, if your father had been a crook, I would have become a cat burglar just to please him."

She reached across the table and took his hand in hers. "I'm glad my father found you."

Tyler stared at her, wondering how it had happened, when it had happened. How in the hell had he managed to do something so stupid, so horrible, as to fall in love with Samantha Dark?

It was a short day in court. After a brief and uneventful afternoon, Samantha and Tyler left the courthouse. Outside in the cold autumn wind, Samantha stopped on the sidewalk. "I'm not going back to the office. I'm spending the rest of the afternoon in the library," she said to him.

He frowned his disapproval. "I really don't think that's a good idea, especially in light of Bones's phone call last night." His frown deepened. "And I still think we need to tell the police."

"What are the police going to do? Right now it's nothing but a threat from an unknown source." She shook her head. They'd argued about getting the police involved last night before going to their separate rooms. She didn't want to have the same argument now. "Tyler, I can't spend every moment of every day in your company for safety's sake. The library is a public place. It's the middle of the afternoon. I'll be fine."

"How will you get home?"

"I'll take a cab." She placed a hand on his arm. She couldn't tell him she needed some time, some distance away from him. In the past two days her emotions had been on a roller-coaster ride and she needed some space to sort things out. "Don't worry, I'll be careful," she added.

"I'll drive you to the library," he replied. She nodded and together they walked toward the car. She got into the passenger seat, then looked at him as he slid in behind the wheel.

He looked exhausted. The effects of the noon break that had pulled the horrible memories from him still showed in his features. She had a feeling he would use the time alone to pull himself back together, to shove those memories into a dark recess of his mind where they wouldn't have the power to haunt him.

It took them only moments to reach the Wilford Public Library, a large old two-story brick building. Tyler pulled up to the curb and Samantha started to get out of the car. Tyler stopped her with a hand on her arm.

"Samantha, please be careful," he said, his dark eyes radiating worry. "Come right home after you finish here."

"I will. You can count on me to be home for dinner." She got out of the car and waited for him to pull away from the curb, then realized he wasn't going anywhere until he saw her safely inside the library doors.

With a parting wave, she ran up the stairs and entered the building. History had it that the Wilford Public Library was the third building constructed in what would eventually become the town of Wilford. Built by the wealthy John Wilford, the founding father, who had wanted his daughter to have all the amenities of city living, the library was a testimony to John Wilford's love of the written word.

Samantha walked past the librarian's counter, where books were checked out and fines were paid. She walked through the rows and rows of books, heading for the stairway that would take her to the second floor.

Upstairs was a lounge of sorts. Tables and chairs were arranged in front of a magazine rack that held a variety of newspapers and magazines. She was alone and had her pick of the tables. She chose one in the corner, where she could work and think undisturbed.

She opened her briefcase and placed a thick manila folder of papers and reports in front of her, but she knew none of the papers contained information on what most played on her mind. Tyler.

Leaning back in the chair, she closed her eyes, remembering how he'd kissed her, how he'd touched her, how he'd loved her the night before. It had been like no experience in her life. It had been beyond her wildest imagination.

Even now, with the odor of musty books assailing her, she could still smell the scent of his clean, masculine skin. And she could still hear his deep moans, his satisfied sighs as he'd loved her.

No, not loved her. She opened her eyes and stared at the paperwork in front of her. *Had sex with her.* It would be a mistake to confuse the two, a mistake she would never make, for it would only lead to heartbreak.

He'd already touched her heart with the story of his mother's murder. As he'd spoken of that night, her heart had ached for the young boy he'd been. She'd wanted to take his pain from him, swallow it up so he would never have to feel it again. That had been unusual for Samantha—to empathize with another's pain. She'd spent too many years wallowing in her own.

Samantha tried to think what it would be like to grow up with no parents, how it would be to spend one's formative years in a foster home. Although she knew there were many good, loving foster parents in the world, she also knew there were some who weren't so loving or so good. She had a feeling Tyler's foster-care experience hadn't been a happy one.

Was a bad parent better than no parent at all? Even

though Samantha had hated her father, had thought him cold and distant, she'd always known that if she got into trouble he would bail her out. She had always felt his presence in her life.

She shook her head, not wanting to explore further thoughts of her father or of Tyler. Her father was dead, and while Tyler was very much alive and she wouldn't mind making love with him again, he was a dead end when it came to anything more than a mutual physical attraction.

Spreading out her paperwork before her, Samantha forced herself to focus on Dominic's case.

She worked for several hours, making notes in margins, considering various scenarios. Other people came and went—men reading magazines, kids doing homework—but Samantha hardly gave them a glance. Rather she stared at crime-scene photos, re-evaluated forensic evidence and tried to find something, anything that would point a finger of suspicion at somebody other than Dominic.

After interviewing Morgan Monroe, her suspicions about him hiring Abigail's killer had waned. Unless the man was the best actor in the world, he truly appeared destroyed by the death of his young bride.

At the moment Samantha's money was riding on Kyle. Although she didn't think the young man had done the job personally, she had a feeling he had something to do with the crime. Unfortunately, she needed a solid link to present to the jury. Her idle speculation wouldn't be allowed or believed.

As her stomach rumbled with hunger, she looked at her watch. Surprised to discover it was almost six o'clock, she packed up her briefcase and headed back down the stairs.

She was on her way to the pay phone to call a cab when she spied her sister checking out several books. She walked up behind her. "You run into the strangest people at the library," she said.

Melissa whirled around, a smile lifting her features and warming Samantha's heart. "Ah, if it isn't the sexy Samantha Dark, defender of justice." Melissa's blue eyes danced and Samantha noticed she looked relaxed—happier than when the two sisters had shared lunch.

"Why aren't you at the courthouse?" Melissa asked as she took the books she'd checked out from the librarian.

"Early court day. I've been upstairs working for the last couple of hours."

Melissa tilted her head, for a moment looking like their mother as Samantha remembered her. "Why here? Why not at the firm?"

Samantha shrugged and the two walked away from the counter. "I thought maybe a change of scenery would help me think."

"I was just about to head down the street to that little Mexican restaurant. Want to have dinner with me?"

Samantha hesitated, thinking of Tyler, who would be waiting for her at home. Immediate irritation swept through her. She wasn't married to Tyler. She wasn't even dating him. Just because they'd slept together once didn't mean she owed him anything. "I'd love to," she agreed. Besides, she still had the hope that she and Melissa would find a closeness again and they certainly couldn't do that by never seeing each other.

"Great!" Melissa flashed her a warm smile and Samantha knew she'd made the right choice.

Together they walked out into the fading light of day.

"So, how's the trial going?" Melissa asked as they headed toward La Casa Cantina.

"Too early to tell. The trial just began yesterday. I probably won't begin the defense case for another week."

"Are you ready?"

"No." Samantha grinned at her sister. "But I'm doing all I can to get ready. Wylie Brooks is working for me, trying to dig up anything I can use to defend Dominic."

Melissa looked at her in surprise. "I thought Wylie had retired."

"Tyler talked him into coming out of retirement to help me."

Their conversation ceased as they entered the dark confines of the restaurant. "How's the divorce coming?" Samantha asked, once they'd been seated and had placed their orders.

"It's not. I stopped the process."

Samantha looked at her sister in surprise. "Why?"

Melissa smiled, her face glowing with happiness. "Bill is trying so hard to make things work out between us. We've been talking...really talking about our problems. I think it's going to be fine. And...I'm going to have a baby. I just found out this morning."

"Oh, Melissa, that's wonderful." Samantha reached across the table and took her sister's hand. "I'm so happy for you."

Melissa laughed and squeezed Samantha's hand. "Me, too." She rubbed her stomach and sighed. "I still don't quite believe it's true, but the doctor assured me that in seven months I'll have a baby."

"Have you told Bill yet?"

Melissa nodded her head. "I told him as soon as I

heard. He's thrilled. I think it's going to work out, Samantha. I really do." She released Samantha's hand.

Samantha felt a flicker of envy sweep through her. A husband. A baby. Those were dreams Samantha had rarely allowed herself. While she believed that deep, abiding love was possible for some people, she'd never quite believed it was possible for her.

"So, tell me about you. Are you and Tyler getting along all right?" Melissa asked.

Samantha grinned. "Well, we haven't killed each other yet."

"That's progress," Melissa replied with a laugh.

Samantha wondered what her sister would say if she knew Samantha and Tyler were not only getting along okay, but had made love the night before. She decided there were some things you didn't share with anyone, not even a sister.

"Samantha, I'm sorry I was so cranky when we had lunch." Melissa looked down at the tabletop. "I was dealing with a lot of things...like Father's death and the idea of divorce."

"And ambivalent feelings toward me," Samantha added.

Melissa looked at her in surprise. Samantha smiled.

"Melissa, I think we need to talk about us. You and me. When Mom was alive, we were so close. After she was gone and as we grew up, we lost that. I want it again, but in order to find it I think we need to talk about why we're angry with each other."

"I'm not angry at you," Melissa protested, but again her gaze didn't quite meet Samantha's.

"Yes, you are," Samantha countered. "Just like I've got a little edge of anger toward you—anger that Father fed." Samantha lowered her voice into a parody of their father's. "'Why can't you be more like your sister? She knows the rules, she abides by them. What's wrong with you, Samantha? Why can't you be more like Melissa'?"

Melissa stared at her in stunned silence, then burst into peals of laughter. "Oh, Samantha, you know what's really funny? He was always saying those same kinds of things to me. Why can't you be smart like Samantha? Even though she makes bad choices, her mind is sharp as a razor while you do nothing but simper and smile."

"He really said that?" Samantha asked in surprise.

"All the time. If he wasn't storming about your escapades, he was talking about your successes. It always felt like everything was about you. His life seemed consumed with you."

Samantha felt as if the world had tilted slightly, as if her take on reality suddenly had a slant that made it difficult for her to keep her balance. "And I always thought everything was about you. Melissa made cheerleader, Melissa made homecoming queen. Everyone loves Melissa—and nobody loves Samantha." Samantha snapped her napkin onto her lap, the anger that always accompanied thoughts of her father sweeping through her like a flame from hell's fire. She looked at Melissa again. "Do you think he was a bastard on purpose?"

Melissa shook her head and smiled sadly. "No, I don't think he knew any better. I think he was so overwhelmed with the idea of raising two little girls alone, he used the only tools he had in his possession—sarcasm, comparison, and coldness. He wasn't a bad man, Samantha. Just inadequate as a father."

"I hate him. Nobody can make me believe he loved me, and I can never forgive him for that." Samantha swallowed against the bitterness that threatened to crawl up her throat.

"Never is a long time," Melissa replied softly.

"You know what they say—'To err is human, to forgive, divine.' Well, I'm only human and I can't forget. Nor can I forgive him."

The waitress appeared with their orders and for a moment the two fell silent. "I lied before," Melissa said when the waitress had left.

Samantha raised an eyebrow. "About what?"

"About being angry with you. I have been angry," she admitted. "Oh, Samantha, why'd you leave? Why'd you leave me all alone? I felt like first Mama abandoned us, then you abandoned me."

Samantha looked away, no longer able to meet Melissa's gaze, where accusation mingled with pain. "I was never leaving you," she answered softly. "It was him. I felt like I was smothering, dying a little piece at a time." She forced herself to look at Melissa. "I was purposely doing dumb things, taking chances that were self-destructive. I had to go, Melissa. I had to leave in order to survive."

Melissa nodded. "I realize that now. I didn't for a long time." This time it was Melissa who reached across the table for Samantha's hand. "It appears the Dark girls have finally grown up."

"It's about damn time," Samantha replied with a grin as she tightly squeezed her younger sister's hand.

Pleasant conversation, laughter and memories accompanied the rest of the meal, made it a time of healing, of forgiving that filled Samantha's soul as effectively as the food sated her appetite.

They had finished eating and split the check when Melissa looked at her watch and gasped. "I've got to run. Bill is coming over to talk about moving back into the house." She wiped her mouth, shoved back from the table and stood. "You need a ride home?"

Samantha shook her head. "I'm fine. Go talk to your husband. I'll keep in touch."

"Please do." With a tremulous smile, Melissa leaned down and hugged Samantha. "I love you, Sammie." She straightened, her smile widening. "Even if I do usually want to pinch off your head."

Samantha laughed, emotional tears hovering too close for comfort. "Get out of here." She watched as her sister left the restaurant, a fullness and warmth pressing around her heart. She and Melissa would still have fights, would never see eye-to-eye on a million issues, but Samantha now knew they were going to be just fine.

She sighed tiredly. Building bridges was hard work. In the past it had always been easier to tear them down. Maybe Melissa was right. Maybe finally, after all these years, Samantha Dark was growing up.

She stood and headed for the rest rooms, where she'd seen a pay phone. She would call a cab and be home within a few minutes. Tyler would probably be irritated that she hadn't come home when she'd told him she would, but surely he would understand when she explained.

After calling for a cab, she went outside to await its arrival. Although it was dark and chilly, the wind had stopped blowing and overhead a million stars winked down at her.

A baby. Melissa was going to have a baby. A wistful ache stole through Samantha. What would it be like to carry the harvest of love? To feel the flutter of life inside?

She pulled her coat collar closer around her neck. She

would probably never know what it was like to be married or pregnant. She shoved the little ache aside. But she would be the best aunt a kid could ever have. "Move over, Auntie Mame," she said to herself with a grin.

A whisper of movement behind her pulled her from her thoughts. Without warning, before she could feel the first clutch of fear, hands shoved her hard from behind. Air whooshed from her lungs as she pitched to the ground, her palms and knees sliding across the sidewalk pavement.

Before she could gain her breath—still reeling with confusion—a blow to her leg caused her to cry out. Then a second blow pounded, with an audible snap. He broke my leg, she thought with wild fear. Still facedown, unable to see her attacker, pain as she'd never before felt shot through her. Darkness flirted at the edges of her mind.

Something hard hit the back of her head. The darkness grew around her and she reached for it. Her last conscious thought was that Tyler was going to be madder than hell.

Chapter 10

When Samantha didn't show up for dinner, Tyler felt the first stir of fear whisper through him. He tamped it down, telling himself she was irresponsible, impetuous and totally unreliable. Why should it surprise him that she was late for dinner?

He waited until after seven, then ate alone. As he ate, he thought back to the noon break, when he'd finally told Samantha about his mother's death. There had been a certain release in finally talking about the horrible day that had changed his life forever and stolen away the one woman who'd truly loved him.

Love. As Samantha had held him, comforted him along the walk through his memories, he'd thought he felt that particular emotion for her. He'd since realized what he'd felt for Samantha had been wrought by the emotional outburst of those memories. It had been gratitude mingled with friendship. Nothing more.

Virginia interrupted his thoughts as she poked her

head into the dining room where Tyler sat alone. "If you have all that you need, I'll be leaving now. I don't intend to stand around here waiting for her to get home."

"Can I ask you something, Virginia?" She nodded and stepped all the way into the room. "Why don't you like Samantha?" Tyler asked.

Virginia frowned, as if made uncomfortable by his question. "It's not exactly that I don't like her. I just don't always approve of her."

Tyler felt a rueful grin cross his face. "That, I can relate to," he agreed easily. "But...it's more than that for you, isn't it?"

Virginia's stern features grew reflective. "Samantha is...has always been..." She paused for a moment as if searching for words. "Difficult," she finally said. "She expects too much from people, makes everyone around her feel inadequate."

Again, reflection stole across her features and she leaned against the counter. "She was always hanging on to me, pulling on my arm, wrapping her arms around my neck, demanding I love her. I wasn't used to children, had never wanted any of my own." Virginia frowned, showing displeasure at her memories. "It was the same with her father. Samantha was always tugging at him, hugging him, demanding he pay attention to her, love her more than he loved anyone else. She was so needy...it made people uncomfortable."

Tyler nodded, oddly saddened by the mental image of a little girl desperate for love. Was it any wonder Samantha had chosen to gain attention in negative ways when the positive ones didn't work?

"Do you need me anymore this evening?" Virginia's voice cut into Tyler's thoughts.

He shook his head. "No, you can go on home. Thanks, Virginia. Dinner was wonderful, as usual."

When Virginia had left, Tyler's thoughts once again turned to Samantha. At least he'd had the pleasure of having his mother—who had been impetuous and reckless, but always loving—for his first fourteen years.

Samantha had had her mother only until she was six; then had apparently been left in the charge of a cold, impersonal man and a housekeeper equally incapable of meeting her need to be loved.

While Melissa had retreated into a shell of perfection, always doing whatever it took to please her father, Samantha had rebelled in all the traditional ways, never realizing the fault wasn't hers, but rather a fault of nature, of fate. Fate had placed her, a needy child, into a houseful of adults who hadn't had the capacity to fill her needs. And where in the hell was she right now? he wondered as he looked at his watch.

The library would be closing in another hour. Surely she wasn't working this late. A call to the library gave him his answer. The librarian told him she'd been there, but had left with Melissa. Tyler relaxed. If she was with Melissa, she would probably be all right. Then, realizing he was worrying about her like some long-suffering husband, he left the kitchen and went upstairs to his bedroom for an early night.

Although exhaustion weighed heavily on him, sleep remained elusive as thoughts of Samantha and the Marcola case continued to plague him.

Reluctantly, he'd begun to believe in Dominic's innocence. There were simply too many inconsistencies, too many facts that added up to something other than mere coincidence. The police had rushed to an arrest, closing the case without a proper investigation. Although Tyler couldn't really fault them; in effect they'd caught Dominic with a smoking gun.

But Tyler had a feeling that Dominic had simply been a pawn in a much larger game—a man caught in the wrong place at the wrong time. Somehow, Tyler knew he and Samantha were missing something—something important. But what?

His head filled with images. Not images from the trial, but of the night he'd held Samantha in his arms, the night she'd surrendered all to him. Why? Why had she chosen to let him be her first?

If he didn't know better, he would believe she'd allowed him to be her first lover specifically to disrupt his sleep, confuse his thoughts.

He'd felt as if it were his first time, too. Each sensation had affected him as if it were a totally new experience.

He turned onto his back, irritated by his thoughts.

He shouldn't be focused on Samantha. He should be thinking of Sarah, who would make him a good wife, who would be a model mother. A woman who would never be late for dinner, never make his stomach twist into knots. A woman with whom he would never achieve the same heights of passion, the soul-searing connection he'd felt with Samantha.

"Dammit." He turned over and punched his pillow. Flipping on the bedside lamp, he sat up, knowing sleep would remain elusive until he knew she was home safe and sound. He grabbed a law journal he'd been reading and turned to the page where he'd left off. Surely she would be home soon, then he could put all inappropriate thoughts of her cleanly and clearly out of his head.

The jarring noise of the phone awoke him, pulling him from the sleep that had finally caught up with him.

He grabbed for the receiver, at the same time looking at the clock next to his bed. Almost one. "Samantha?" he said into the phone.

"Tyler. It's me."

He relaxed and sent a prayer upward as he heard her voice.

"Where in the hell are you?" he demanded as anger toppled fear.

"That's what I was calling for, to see if you would mind coming to pick me up."

"Where are you?" he repeated.

"When I tell you, don't freak out. Everything is fine now, and the doctor says my leg will heal without any problems."

"Your leg?" Tyler had a vision of her sexy, long legs. "What happened to your leg?"

"It's broken. But the taxi driver was more concerned about my head."

Tyler gripped the phone so tightly he thought he heard the plastic crack beneath his grasp. "Your head? Never mind, I don't want to know. Just tell me where you are."

"The hospital."

"I'll be there in five minutes." Tyler hung up the phone and cursed soundly as he dressed. Questions raced through his head. What in the hell had happened? A car accident? Taxi drivers here in Wilford didn't share the same traits as those drivers in big cities. Still, he could easily imagine Samantha sitting in the back of a cab in one of her impossibly short skirts, the driver ogling the rearview mirror instead of watching traffic. Accidents happened. Especially when Samantha was involved.

It took Tyler only minutes to drive to the Wilford hospital. He walked into the emergency entrance and was told that Samantha had been placed in room 212. The moment he reached the second floor, he heard her.

"No way, Doc. There's no way I'm staying overnight." Her words rang out loud and clear in the silent semidarkness of the hallway. A nurse came out of the room, looking harried. She flashed Tyler a grim smile, then continued past him.

Drawing a deep breath, promising himself he wouldn't get upset or angry, Tyler entered room 212. Samantha sat on the edge of the bed, clad in a loose-fitting hospital gown. A massive, pristine white cast covered her lower left leg.

She gave Tyler what appeared to be a wide, drunken grin as she saw him. "Ah, there's my ride. Tell them, Tyler. Tell them I can't possibly stay here tonight. I've got court first thing in the morning."

Tyler looked at Dr. Bumgarten, who'd been the Dark family physician for as long as Tyler had been around. The old man looked frazzled, his glasses slightly askew and white hair standing on end.

"Samantha, you've had a shock. I'd feel more comfortable if you'd remain here for the night," Dr. Bumgarten replied. He looked at Tyler as if for help. "Surely the court would grant a postponement under the circumstances."

"What exactly are the circumstances?" Tyler asked.

"It's no big deal," Samantha said as she stood and swayed as if slightly woozy. Dr. Bumgarten grabbed her arm to steady her. She flashed him a grateful smile, then looked back at Tyler. "I was mugged."

"Mugged?" Tyler eyed her in surprise. Muggings were rare on the streets of Wilford.

"Like I said, it's no big deal." She clomped across the room and picked up a pile of clothing, then headed for the bathroom. "And there's no way I'm going to ask for a postponement or spend the night here. I'll be out in a minute, then we can go home," she said to Tyler, and disappeared into the bathroom, shutting the door behind her.

Dr. Bumgarten sighed and ran a hand through his thin hair, causing it to stand at attention atop his head. "She's as stubborn as Jamison ever was," he said, then sank into the chair beside the bed.

"So, tell me exactly what happened," Tyler prompted, feeling as if he'd walked into a play during the third act. "Samantha said something about being mugged."

Dr. Bumgarten shook his head. "This was no mugging. Her purse wasn't stolen, and no mugger I know shoves their victim from behind, then hits them in the leg hard enough to break bones."

Tyler sucked in his breath. "Is that what happened?" Tyler's own legs ached in response. "Did she see who it was?"

The doctor shook his head again. "All she remembers is being shoved. Apparently she fell to the pavement where she was hit first in the leg, then in the back of her head. She blacked out."

"Where did this happen?"

"In front of the Mexican restaurant on Main. She'd called for a cab and stepped out front to wait. The taxi driver pulled up and frightened off the attacker. It was the driver who brought her in."

Tyler fought off an icy chill that threatened to climb up his spine. The doctor was right. This didn't sound like a garden-variety mugging. It sounded like attempted murder. "What's the prognosis?"

A ghost of a smile whispered across the doctor's features. "Not good for the man who did this to her. But she'll be fine. The blow to the back of her head was a glancing one. I've got her on some pretty heavy-duty painkillers for her leg."

Tyler nodded, realizing the drugs were probably the reason for her dopey grin when he'd entered the room. At that moment Samantha came out of the bathroom. "Thanks, Doc, for all your help," she said. Neither the doctor nor Tyler mentioned to her that her blouse was buttoned wrong or that her skirt was twisted crookedly. "Come on, Tyler. Let's go home." Without waiting for him, she clomped out of the room.

"I want to see her in a week to check on that leg," Dr. Bumgarten said. "When those painkillers wear off, she's probably going to be pretty miserable."

"I have a feeling I will be, too," Tyler muttered wryly. Thanking the doctor, he hurried out after Samantha.

"Thanks for coming to take me home," she said to him as he caught up with her. She flashed him a quicksilver smile. "Waiting for cabs can be hazardous to your health."

Tyler said nothing. He refused to make light of the situation, but knew the hospital parking lot was no place to conduct the kind of conversation he intended to have with her when they got home.

He helped her into his car, the cast on her leg making her unnaturally clumsy and off balance. She got in, leaned her head back against the seat and closed her eyes.

She remained that way until they were nearly home.

When Tyler turned into the driveway, she opened her eyes and gazed at him. "You're mad, aren't you? I hated to wake you up but I didn't know who else to call to come and get me."

Tyler parked the car, then turned and looked at her incredulously. "You think I'm mad because you woke me up?" He frowned at her, then realized that would only add to her misperception. "Come on, let's get you inside."

He helped her into the house where both of them immediately went to the study. As Samantha sank into one of the wing chairs, Tyler lit a fire in the fireplace. When he turned back to her, he smiled. "Samantha, I'm not angry because you woke me up."

"That's a relief." She cast him a crooked smile. "I feel too good to have anyone angry with me. Those pills the doctor gave me have given me a nice euphoric cushion."

"We do have to talk about what happened. You realize it wasn't just a simple mugging."

"I know. I also have a clue as to who was behind the attack," she said. "And I don't think it has anything to do with the Marcola case."

He looked at her in surprise. "Then what? Who?"

She pulled something from her pocket and held it out to him. It was a silver money clip with the initials R.B. engraved on it. "That was on the ground next to me when I came to. Rick Brennon," she said.

Tyler thought of the burly man he'd tangled with at the Devil's Kitchen. Was it possible the attack on Samantha had been payback?

Samantha grinned at him, her eyes slightly glazed from the painkillers. "I guess maybe Brennon thought he'd be getting back at you by hurting me. Silly, huh?"

"Samantha, this is nothing to joke about," he replied, his blood hot as he thought of Brennon assaulting Samantha. "Did you make a police report? Give the police this information?"

She nodded. "Sheriff Caldwell came to the hospital and took a report. I didn't tell him about finding the money clip, although I did tell him I thought Brennon might be involved."

Tyler looked down at the clip in his hand. "I knew the man wasn't exactly a mental giant, but this seems even too stupid for Brennon—to drop a calling card at the scene of a crime." He frowned. It just didn't feel right. Brennon was a bar brawler, not the type to hit a defenseless woman in some sort of retribution.

"Personally, I prefer to think whoever attacked me wanted to stop me from proceeding on the Marcola case," Samantha said, her eyes having difficulty focusing on Tyler. "Because that would mean whoever it is, is afraid of my legal skills. That they think I might succeed in proving Dominic innocent and the case would be reopened. That's what I like to think." As her words slurred, Tyler realized the full brunt of the pain pills must be hitting her.

"Come on, Ms. Legal Eagle, it's time for you to go to sleep." He stood and helped her out of the chair. When they reached the foot of the stairs, Samantha paused, sighing as she eyed her destination at the top.

Without hesitation, Tyler scooped her up in his arms. He tensed as she immediately wound her arms around his neck and laid her head against his chest. "Thanks," she murmured. Her breath played warm and sweet against his throat. "I want you to be the first one to sign my cast," she said.

He didn't reply. He carried her into her room, pulled

down the covers on the bed and placed her there, but she didn't release her grasp on him. "Stay with me," she whispered, and attempted to pull him down next to her on the bed. "Oh, Tyler, when I got hit from behind, I was so scared. I thought I was going to die."

"Shh, you're safe now." Gently, he unwound her arms from around his neck, then removed her shoes. His gaze fell on the cast and he imagined Rick Brennon hitting her with something…a bat…a pipe…hitting her sweet, soft flesh so hard it broke the bones within.

Rage tore through Tyler—a killing, blinding rage. If the sheriff didn't arrest Brennon, if the legal system somehow failed, then Tyler would seek his own particular brand of justice. He didn't care how long it took, sooner or later somebody would pay for Samantha's pain.

"Tyler?" Samantha's voice was soft, blurred by the sleep-inducing drugs.

"What?" He pulled the sheet up around her.

"I'm glad we made love." A smile curved her lips as her eyes drifted closed. "I…I wouldn't have wanted to die without doing that." Her words faded and with a sigh she surrendered herself to sleep.

Tyler watched her for a long time. He stood next to her bed, noting the spill of her hair against the pillowcase, the tiny veins across her eyelids that made her look so vulnerable.

He loved her. Hopelessly. Helplessly. He loved her as deeply as he'd ever loved before. The knowledge filled him with horror, twisted his gut. He didn't want to love her, was afraid of feeling that emotion for her.

He left the room but didn't go far. He leaned against the wall in the hallway, drawing in deep breaths as he fought an internal war between love and fear. Loving

Samantha scared him more than anything he'd ever experienced.

He'd sworn to himself years before that he would never allow fate to play havoc with his heart again. He'd sworn he would never love a woman who took chances, lived so fully, and rode the edge of risk. He'd loved a woman like that once, and she'd wound up dead. He would never put himself through that again.

Sooner or later he was going to have to come to a decision. He was going to have to either learn how to hate Samantha, or sell her his half of Justice Inc. and leave her and this town behind.

"There's got to be a mistake." Samantha looked at the big, bald old man sitting across from her. "I could have sworn it was Rick Brennon who attacked me."

Wylie Brooks shrugged his massive shoulders. "Not unless the man can be at two places at one time. As you see in my report, at the time of your assault, he was in attendance at his niece's wedding. More than thirty witnesses placed him there."

Samantha set that particular report aside and thumbed through the others Wylie had brought with him. "Anything interesting in Abigail's background?"

Wylie shook his head. "Nothing that jumped out at me. Before marrying Morgan Monroe, she was living alone, dating your client and working as a waitress out at the country club. No scandals that I could find, no skeletons to rattle, no potential suspects to point to."

Samantha sighed dispiritedly. "Thanks, Wylie. I'll look these over and if I think of anything else I need, I'll call you."

After Wylie left the office, Samantha leaned back in her chair and released another long, weary sigh. The day after her assault, Samantha had shown up in court, only to have the judge, despite her protests, grant a week's delay in the proceedings for the benefit of her health.

"Ms. Dark, there is no way you can be at your best today after what you experienced last night," Judge Halloran had explained. Although Samantha had argued with him, the judge had been adamant. Samantha had gone home and spent the next two days in bed, realizing Judge Halloran had been right. Her body ached and her mind felt numb.

This morning she'd awakened knowing it was time to get back to work. Now she had two goals—to get Dominic off and to find whoever had tried to kill her.

She scanned Wylie's reports, searching for something, anything that could be used in Dominic's defense. She'd assigned Wylie to getting any and all background material on Abigail, Kyle and Georgia Monroe, and Rick Brennon.

Brennon's report read like a rap sheet. She noticed that on more than one occasion Brennon's arresting officer had been Dominic Marcola. In and out of trouble since his teenage years, Brennon had more than enough reason to frame Dominic. And if he framed Dominic, he wouldn't want the man to get off because that would reopen the investigation.

It made sense to think that Brennon had attacked her, hoping to get her pulled from the case. In all probability, if she dropped Dominic's case, an overworked, underpaid public defendant would take over, making Dominic's chances of acquittal virtually nil.

But Brennon hadn't attacked her. The proof was in Wylie's report before her. And if he hadn't done it, why had somebody tried to make it look as if he had? To provide a false lead?

She leaned back in the chair and placed her leg with the cast on top of the desk. Although she'd only had the cast on for three days, already her leg had started the itching that indicated healing. She drew a pencil from her drawer and shoved it beneath the edge of the cast, trying to hit the place that itched with the eraser end of the pencil.

"I don't remember that being on your list of written instructions from Dr. Bumgarten."

Samantha looked up to see Tyler standing in her doorway. She blushed, pulled the pencil out of the cast, and set her leg back on the floor. "It itches."

"There are some itches best left unscratched."

Samantha grinned. "Not as far as I'm concerned. I'm a firm believer in scratching where it itches." Her smile faltered as Tyler didn't reply, didn't smile. He'd been cool and distant since the night of her attack—although he'd insisted he drive her to and from work, and that she not go anyplace else unless she had somebody with her. It had surprised Samantha how much his aloofness bothered her.

"You ready to head home?" he asked.

She nodded. "Just let me gather up some paperwork."

"I'll wait right out here." He disappeared from her vision and she quickly shoved Wylie's reports and Dominic's thick file into her briefcase.

"All set," she told Tyler a moment later as she met him by Edie's desk. "Good night, Edie," she said to the red-haired receptionist. "Don't work too late."

Edie laughed. "Honey, work is about the most exciting thing in my life these days." She waved to them as they went out the door and into the cool twilight shadows of approaching night.

"I saw Wylie a little while ago," Tyler said as they got into his car.

"He came by to give me some reports."

"Anything worthwhile?"

"Not really, although I now know Rick Brennon wasn't the one who did this to me. While I was being attacked, Rick was at a wedding reception on the other side of town. As far as the other reports are concerned, I haven't had a chance to look them over yet, but Wylie said nothing jumped out at him."

They fell silent—not the companionable silence they had enjoyed in the past, but one filled with tension. Samantha endured it until they got to the house, then spoke. "Tyler, are you mad at me?"

"Have you done something that I should be mad about?" he countered.

"Not that I'm aware of, but I don't always know when I'm being irritating or maddening."

Tyler parked and shut off the engine, then turned to her.

In his dark gaze, she saw irritation, ire…and a flame of something she knew she shouldn't disturb: desire. It burned in his eyes, warmed her from the inside out. She knew she was a fool to want it, but she did.

She leaned toward him, intent on touching him, wanting to place her lips against his until he moaned. In a single fluid movement, he got out of the car.

"I hope Virginia fixed something good for dinner. I'm starved." His voice had a forced lightness as he helped her out of the car.

"Me, too," she replied. Although she wasn't speaking about dinner. She was starved for his touch, wanted a repeat of their lovemaking. It had nothing to do with love, she thought, as they made their way to the front door. It had to do with pleasure. She could make love without being in love, she told herself. She stumbled as her head filled with the memory of the single night they had shared. Yes, she wanted to be in his arms again, feel the joy of their union.

The house smelled of spaghetti sauce and garlic when they walked in. Virginia met them at the door, obviously pleased to have them home for the meal on time for a change. "I'll just set it on the table," she said.

As Virginia bustled to finish preparing the meal, Tyler and Samantha settled in at the table. When Samantha's father had been alive, all meals had been eaten in the formal dining room. Samantha was grateful that she and Tyler preferred the cozy confines of the kitchen. Here, the table was a smaller, round one, making the meal more intimate. Samantha liked the fact that she sat close enough to Tyler to smell his scent, to see into the depths of his eyes when they spoke.

As Virginia served them, Samantha looked down at her plate in sudden confusion. She liked the fact that she and Tyler sat together each evening at the table, sharing pieces of their day, bantering like a comfortable married couple. When had that happened? When had she begun to look forward to this time with Tyler? How had the man she'd wanted to hate, the man she couldn't wait to force out of the firm and out of her life, become such an integral part of her life?

It was crazy to think a relationship with Tyler could go anywhere. Absurd to even think a long-term relationship with Tyler was possible. She could never be the kind of woman he wanted. So, why was she so certain that before the night was over she would be in his arms? Why did she know with heart certainty that they were going to make love before this night was through?

Chapter 11

It worried Tyler that Samantha was so silent during their meal. In the past several weeks, their dinners had been accompanied by her easy chatter. They debated legal issues, argued past decisions rendered, and rarely suffered a moment's quiet while eating.

Tonight, silence reigned. She concentrated on her meal, obviously filled with thoughts she preferred not to share. What was brewing in her pretty head?

The ticktock of the kitchen clock seemed unnaturally loud and he could hear the faint but steady rhythm of Samantha's breathing.

"You're terribly quiet," he finally said, breaking the oppressive stillness.

She looked up and flashed him a quick smile. "Just thinking."

"Anything you want to share?"

She hesitated, as if weighing options, then shook her head. "No, nothing important." She toyed with her spaghetti, her fork twirling and untwirling strands of pasta. She looked at him again, her expression thoughtful. "Do you ever think about where you would be now if my father hadn't met you when he did?"

"I know where I'd be—in jail."

She nodded, her brow wrinkled in thought. "I sometimes wonder where I would be now if I hadn't left Wilford years ago."

Tyler smiled at her. "Probably in the cell next to mine."

She laughed, the low throaty sound shooting a thrill of desire through Tyler. "You're probably right," she agreed. Her smile faded and her gaze met his. "You know, I wasn't half as bad as everyone thought I was." Her eyes shone with an intensity that touched his heart.

"I know."

A teasing light stole into her eyes. "Although sometimes I have wicked thoughts that I know would make you blush if you knew what they were."

Tyler felt the beginning of a responding blush heat his hairline. Her laughter surrounded him once again—stimulating, provocative. Life with Samantha would never be dull or boring.

Once again he felt a desperate need to distance himself from her. He stood and took his plate to the sink.

"Oh, Tyler, sometimes you are so predictable," she teased.

He rinsed his plate, wondering why "predictable" sounded so much like "boring." "You make 'predictable' sound like a negative trait," he said as he placed his dishes in the dishwasher.

"On the contrary, I find it an admirable trait." She got up and walked toward him.

How was it possible for her to look so damned sexy

with a heavy cast on her leg? he wondered as she stopped directly in front of him. He tensed, both worried and excited by the little smile that played at the corners of her mouth.

"There is something nice about 'predictable,'" she said softly. "For example, I know if I do this—" she wrapped her arms around his waist and pressed her body against his "—I know I'll feel your heart quicken against mine."

Tyler tried to stop his body's response to hers, but it was as impossible as attempting to stop his next breath. "Samantha...what are you doing?"

"I'm showing you how predictable you are." She pressed her lips against his throat. "And when I kiss you here, you tighten your arms around me."

Tyler cursed inwardly as he felt his arms pulling her closer, more tightly against him. Boring? Predictable? She squealed in surprise as he scooped her up in his arms. "What are you doing?" she asked breathlessly as he headed for the stairs.

He grinned at her. "Showing you just how unpredictable I can be."

He carried her upstairs to his bed, wanting to make love to her against the backdrop of his navy sheets, in the room where he'd dreamed of her on so many lonely nights.

As their lips met, all restraint, all control shattered between them. The first time they'd made love, it had been slow, careful—a time of discovery and wonder. This time, there were no gentle caresses, no building of fire and heat. The fire flamed out of control, the heat exploding as they tore at each other's clothing.

He knew it was a mistake. He could forgive himself the error of making love to Samantha once, but this was sheer madness that could lead nowhere. Still, these thoughts did nothing to temper the need that roared through him like a blazing inferno.

Later. Later he would regain some distance. Later he would learn how to deny to himself and to her his desire for her. For now, he simply wanted to love her.

They moved like two starving animals, falling on each other with hungry kisses and feverish caresses. As Tyler entered her, rationality vanished and he lost himself in the sweet heat of her.

Afterward, they remained in each other's arms, their breaths slowing as their hearts sought a more normal rhythm. Tyler felt the need to say something, to talk about the spontaneous combustion that had just occurred between them, but he didn't know exactly what to say.

He couldn't distance himself from her completely as long as the Marcola trial was going on. He'd promised her he would help with Dominic's defense. And he couldn't promise himself he wouldn't make love to her again and again if given the opportunity. However, he knew it would be best for them both if they could finish the trial without falling into bed another time.

"Samantha?" He pulled his arm out from beneath her and sat up. She didn't answer. He reached out and turned on the bedside lamp, and saw that she was sleeping—as soundly, as peacefully as a babe.

He watched her for a long moment, memorizing each and every feature that made her distinctly Samantha. The strong jawline, the arrogant arch of each pale eyebrow, the nose with its impudent upturn—all made the face of the woman he loved. But the knowledge of his love for her filled him with alternating joy and despair; he had promised himself long ago that no woman would own his heart, that he would never again make himself vulnerable to losing a woman he loved.

He closed his eyes, a vision of his mother invading his mind. Laughing. She was almost always laughing, as if life were a carnival and she was just along for the thrill of the rides.

It was Tyler who had reminded her to pay the electric bills, who had made out grocery lists and cooked meals. It was Tyler who had spent hours waiting for her return, wondering if she would come back safe and sound. And the one night he hadn't waited—the one night he'd decided to be late and make her wait for him—she had died.

He couldn't handle feeling that kind of pain…that kind of rage again. He wouldn't. And loving Samantha made him afraid that one day he would have to face those feelings again. She was simply too impetuous, and so filled with life, he feared she made herself a target for fate.

Silently, not wanting to rouse her but unable to remain near her any longer, he crept from the bed. He pulled on his slacks and left the room.

Downstairs in the study, he started a fire, then poured himself a brandy and sat down. As he stared into the flames, emotions battled in his heart. He envied Samantha her peaceful sleep. Apparently she suffered no moral dilemmas, was able to separate their mutual physical attraction and any pretense of love.

For ages women had complained of men's capacity to make love without being in love. Apparently Tyler was an anomaly; he couldn't imagine making love without feeling it in his heart, in his soul.

He tried to envision himself making love to Sarah. She was an attractive woman. He'd kissed her before, found kissing her pleasant enough, but lacking the intense response he felt just thinking of kissing Samantha.

He took a sip of the brandy and closed his eyes. It seemed impossible to believe that he'd once considered proposing to Sarah. He realized now that the idea of marriage to her had seemed attractive because he didn't love her. He knew she would make him a good wife and his heart would never have to be vulnerable.

He also realized that now, marriage to Sarah wasn't an option. He couldn't cheat her like that—marry her with no love in his heart, commit to her when his heart was committed to another. He frowned, refusing to consider the depth of his feelings for Samantha.

"What time is it?"

Samantha's voice pulled him from his thoughts. He turned to see her standing in the doorway. Clad in her long, silk navy robe, with her hair tousled and her lips still swollen from his kisses, she looked so sexy it made him ache. "Not late. Just after eight."

She walked over to the window and peered out. "It's disconcerting when it gets dark so early in the evening." She turned back and looked at him. "Would it bother you if I worked for a little while in here?"

"Not at all," he lied. Of course, it would bother him. Everything about her bothered him. He sipped his brandy and watched as she retrieved her briefcase from the kitchen, then opened it and took out a handful of papers. She curled up in the chair across from him and began to read.

He watched her covetously, wondering if there would ever come a day when he tired of looking at her. He didn't think so. Hers was a face filled with character and emotion, always changing, always beautiful, but never the same.

It wasn't just her physical attributes that touched him. He admired her intelligence, loved the vulnerability she tried to hide behind a layer of bravado, and was touched by her utter loyalty.

In one of their many conversations over dinner, she'd told him about her childhood escapes to the cemetery, where Jeb Marcola had soothed her anger, hugged away her tears. Tyler knew it was loyalty, the need to repay an old debt that drove her to want to help Jeb's son.

He frowned and took another sip of his drink, then once again stared into the flickering fire. He'd promised he would help her with the Marcola trial, and he would keep that promise. But once the trial was over, he intended to leave.

He would sell out to her, pack up his bags and start over. The idea was not appealing, but it was far more appealing than remaining here and loving her. That simply couldn't be an option.

Samantha broke into his thoughts. "Did Melissa tell you she's pregnant?"

"No, she didn't. Although she called to tell me to stop her divorce proceedings." Tyler looked at her. She'd placed her paperwork on the floor next to her chair and was staring into the fire as if hypnotized.

"You ever think about having kids?" she asked, her gaze still transfixed.

"No." A tightness grew in his chest. His answer was a lie. Sometimes in the vulnerable moments just before sleep or just upon awakening, he longed for a family. But it was a dream he never let take hold of him, knew he could never realize. "I decided a long time ago that with my background, I wasn't a good risk as father material."

She finally looked at him, her brown eyes thoughtful. "What do you mean...with your background?"

His fingers tightened around the stem of his brandy glass. "I loved my mother. She was all I had when I was younger. But I haven't idealized her in death." He paused for a moment to sip his drink. "She wasn't a good parent. Oh, she wasn't abusive or anything like that. She was forgetful, ruled by impulse. When she remembered she was a mother, she was good at it. The problem was, she often didn't remember."

"But that doesn't mean you'd make the same mistakes," Samantha countered. She stared into the fire. "If I had children, I wouldn't parent like my father did. I'd make sure not a minute passed that they didn't know they were smart, and wonderful, and loved." A smile curved her lips and her features softened. "That's the way my mother was."

"You have good memories of her?"

She nodded, her hair shining in the firelight. "My mother filled the house with laughter. She was always either laughing or singing." She wrapped her arms around her shoulders as if to hug the memory closer. "I remember my father once saying that she was one of those special people in the world, that being with her made everyone else feel special."

"Your father must have loved her very much."

She turned her head to look at Tyler once again, her features registering surprise. Tilting her head, she thought for a moment, then nodded slowly. "Yes, I suppose he did."

"Just another example of loving, then losing somebody," Tyler observed, bitterness creeping into his voice.

Samantha continued to gaze at him. "Is that why

you've never married? Because you're afraid of losing the person you love?" Tyler didn't reply. She laughed, a low chuckle that lacked real mirth. "Aren't we a pair? Both of us pretending not to have hearts when the real truth is our hearts are so wounded we can't trust again."

"I'm not afraid of anything," Tyler answered tersely. "I haven't married because I haven't met a woman I could abide living with for any length of time. What's your excuse?"

She grinned cockily. "I'm not married because I haven't found a man who could abide living with me for any length of time." The smile fell away. "Besides, I've decided I don't want a man in my life, but I would like children someday."

"Samantha, you might be able to accomplish many things, but children without a man I don't think even *you* can achieve," he said dryly.

"I need a man for conceiving, but not for anything else," she returned.

Tyler looked at her in horror. Had that been the sole reason she'd slept with him?

"No," she declared softly, as if she knew exactly what thought had flitted in his head. "Although I have no doubt that we'd make beautiful babies together, you don't have to worry. I'm on birth-control pills. I knew eventually I'd be ready for sex, but I'm not ready for children yet."

"Then why did you sleep with me?" The question fell from his lips without his volition.

Her gaze didn't waver from his. "Because I wanted to. Because even though I find you one of the most irritating men I've ever known, I've always been attracted to you."

She stared into the fire again. "Because while the rest

of the high-school girls were having fantasies about the star football player or the latest rock star, I was having fantasies about you. Just don't let it go to your head, okay?'' She stood. ''I'm going to bed. I'll see you in the morning.'' Without waiting for his reply, she left the study.

Tyler wished he hadn't asked. The idea of her lying in bed, fantasizing about making love with him, touched his heart. She'd been an unloved young woman and he'd been her fantasy. But a fantasy could rarely sustain itself in the cold glare of reality.

He leaned his head back and closed his eyes, trying to imagine Samantha as a mother. She would be a good mother. Like her own mother, she would fill her house with laughter and love, nurturing her child as she'd wanted to be nurtured. He sat up and shoved the evocative images from his mind.

Samantha's father had broken her heart and he knew with certainty that she would never make that kind of mistake with her own children.

Tyler might have been her fantasy once. But he would never become her reality. He knew that if she made the mistake of falling in love with him, he would become just another man who'd betrayed her…just another man who'd broken her heart.

Samantha stood on the balcony in her mother's bedroom. The brisk prewinter-night air whipped her hair around her head and chilled her body through her thin robe. But, she felt she needed the cold clean air to help clarify the thoughts swirling in her head.

The conversation with Tyler had unsettled her. She picked through the remnants of his words, concentrating on the least threatening statement he'd made: "Your father must have loved her very much."

The moment Tyler had said those words, half-forgotten memories had shifted into focus. She remembered a particular breakfast, with all of them around the table. Her mother had been chattering, describing a women's club meeting to Jamison in vivid, comic detail. What Samantha suddenly remembered clearest of all was the expression on her father's face as he'd listened to his wife. Loving indulgence…utter devotion.

That memory recalled others. The sound of her parents' laughter from their bedroom…the secretive looks they would exchange…the way they touched frequently.

He'd loved her. Completely. Desperately. Awe swept through Samantha as the memories of her parents' relationship became clearer in her mind. And while their mother had been alive, Jamison had loved his daughters.

Tears burned Samantha's eyes. Her father's arms surrounding her, his lips pressing a kiss on her forehead before she fell asleep. Sitting on his shoulders when they'd gone to a circus. He'd loved his daughters when his wife had been alive. So what had happened? How had it all changed?

For the first time Samantha wondered if it was possible to love somebody so much that when they died, they took with them the best of the person they left behind. Had that happened to her father? Had his mourning been so intense, so deep that he couldn't face the two little girls left behind with him? Had she and Melissa reminded him daily of his loss, making loving them too difficult to bear?

And was that what had happened to Tyler? Had his

mother's death taken with it the best of him—his capacity to love?

She swiped at the tears that flowed down her cheeks and stepped back into the bedroom. She closed the balcony door and carefully locked it, then drew the curtains across the door. If only she could close her heart off as easily.

She'd once feared herself incapable of love. She'd taken her father's rejection of her to mean that she wasn't fit to be loved. But now, for the first time, she realized her father's treatment had not been a reflection of her, but rather a sickness of his own that had little to do with her.

As this final piece of knowledge clicked into place, she realized she loved Tyler. Perhaps had been in love with him for years. Always, before, the thought of being in love had filled her with fear—the dread of being vulnerable, of getting hurt. This time, it glowed in her heart, warming her from within.

She loved. And she was worth loving. Now, all she had to do was convince Tyler of that fact.

Chapter 12

The following day there was little time for declarations of love or thoughts of her private life. Tyler, coming downstairs late, missed breakfast and seemed preoccupied. Although Samantha's new realization of her love for him ached with the need to be voiced, she knew the timing wasn't right.

Once they got to the firm, he disappeared up the stairs to his office and Samantha went into hers. Within minutes, all thoughts of Tyler and love were shoved aside as she focused on Dominic's case, which would resume the next day.

She knew the prosecution probably had a day or two left of their case in chief, then it would be her turn to present for the defense.

Although she'd managed to poke some holes in the prosecution's theory, she worried that she hadn't done enough to promote reasonable doubt.

Dominic's life weighed heavy on her mind. She had

little to present to the jury, nothing substantial that might make a difference when they deliberated. Old boyfriends were always good for muddying the waters when a young woman was murdered. Unfortunately, Dominic was the old boyfriend.

She sighed in frustration, then jumped as a knock sounded on her door. "Come in."

Edie entered, a foam take-out carton and a can of cola in her hand. "It's after one and you haven't eaten lunch. I got you a roast beef and cheese on white and a soda." She set the sandwich and the drink on the desk.

Samantha smiled. "Thanks Edie. That was really thoughtful." She opened the container and gestured for Edie to sit in the chair opposite the desk. "Sit down, visit with me for a minute."

"Actually, I can't take the credit for your lunch. Tyler came down a little while ago and told me if you hadn't eaten yet, then I should order you something."

"Did he eat?" Samantha asked, trying to decide if she should be touched or irritated by his mothering.

"He was on his way to a late-lunch meeting with a client."

Samantha nodded, deciding not to look a gift horse in the mouth. She eyed the woman who had been a part of her life for so long. "Why aren't you married, Edie?" Relationships suddenly seemed fascinating to Samantha.

Edie shrugged. "Just not in the cards for me, I guess."

"Were you ever in love?" In all the years Samantha had known her, she'd never heard Edie mention dating or having any sort of relationship with anyone. It seemed curious. Although a bit colorful, Edie was attractive, and possessed a huge, loving heart.

"I was in love...but he was unavailable." Edie looked down at the floor, as if embarrassed by the admission.

"Married?" Samantha asked softly.

"I...I didn't realize the depth of his commitment," she replied, then stood. "I'd better get back to my desk." She left, closing the door behind her.

Samantha stared at the door, sympathy swelling inside her. It was a shame. Edie would have made a loving, caring wife. She'd certainly been a loving, caring surrogate mother to Samantha and Melissa. Too bad she hadn't fallen in love with a man who could return that love. Too bad she hadn't had a family of her own.

By the time Samantha finished her lunch, the conversation with Edie was forgotten as she once again focused her attention on the Marcola trial.

She'd lined up her first few witnesses, all friends of Dominic who had offered to be character witnesses. A beginning, but a weak one at best. What she needed more than anything was one of those Perry Mason moments. She closed her eyes, imagining the actual guilty person on the stand crumbling beneath her brilliant questioning.

She snapped her eyes back open, shaking her head ruefully. It was a nice fantasy. Unfortunately she didn't have a clue who the real murderer might be.

At four o'clock, Edie poked her head in the door to tell Samantha that Wylie Brooks had arrived with a handful of new reports.

"Wylie." Samantha stood to greet the bald-headed private investigator. "I certainly hope you have something more interesting than the last batch of reports you brought me."

He grinned and handed her a sheaf of papers. "I think you'll find a few points of interest in these."

Samantha perked up at his words. She sat down and riffled through the reports. "Sit down and tell me what you discovered."

He shook his head, a sheepish grin stealing across his features. "I can't stay. I've got a plane to catch. I'm heading to Mexico on a little fishing trip."

"Now?" Samantha frowned in dismay. "But what if I need something from you?"

"I told both you and Tyler that I'd do what I could to help you, but nothing is going to make me postpone this trip. It's been planned for the better part of six months. Besides—" he gestured to the papers in front of her "—I've done all I can do for you. Those contain everything I could learn about Georgia and Kyle Monroe. You've already got the background stuff on Rick Brennon and Morgan Monroe. That's everything you asked me for."

"You're right." Samantha sighed. "There's probably nothing more you can do for me." She stood and shook his hand. "Thanks, Wylie, for all your help. I know this isn't the way you planned to spend your retirement."

"A fishing pole in one hand, a beer in the other. That's my idea of retirement."

Samantha laughed. "Have a good trip, and happy fishing."

As soon as he left, Samantha sat down and began to read the reports. Within minutes she found the facts Wylie thought would be of interest to her. Excitement bubbled inside her. Grabbing the pertinent papers, she left her office.

"Is Tyler back yet?" she asked Edie.

"No. He hasn't come back from lunch."

"Did he say where he was going?"

"He mentioned the country club," Edie replied.

"Call me a cab," Samantha said, then raced back into her office and grabbed her coat.

A few minutes later, sitting in the back of a taxi, Samantha read and reread the report on Georgia Monroe, wondering if she was making a big deal out of nothing.

She needed to talk to Tyler, tell him what Wylie had discovered, see if her thoughts were completely out in left field, or were directly on track.

Vaguely she wondered who the client was that Tyler was wining and dining at the club. Surely whoever it was would understand her interruption. Dominic's life hung in the balance and she wanted to bounce her scenario off Tyler as soon as possible.

When the cab pulled up in front of the club, she jumped out. "Wait here," she said. "I might be a few minutes, but I'll be back."

She didn't want to send the taxi away in case Tyler had already left. And if he was still here, she would bounce her idea off him, then leave him to deal with his client.

As she walked into the luxury dining area, she was overly conscious of the cast on her leg, the mustard that had leaked out of her sandwich and onto her blouse, and the fact that as usual her hair was a tangled mess.

She pulled her coat closer around her, hoping to hide the mustard stain. She raked a hand through her hair as the hostess eyed her with a hint of disdain. "Don't worry, I'm not staying long," she said to the perfectly coiffed woman. She spied Tyler seated with an older, distinguished-looking man.

He looked up and saw her, his eyes widening in surprise. She waved to him. He excused himself and hurried toward her, a frown puckering his forehead. "Samantha...what's going on? What are you doing here?" He took her by the arm and pulled her away from the hostess.

"Wylie came by and gave me some background reports. I found something interesting in one of them—"

"Can't this wait?" he interrupted. "I'm in the middle of something important here." His voice was snappish, his features taut with tension.

Samantha stared at him, surprised by his obvious irritation with her. "I'm sorry." She took a step backward. "This was thoughtless of me." She turned to leave.

"Samantha, wait!" She didn't stop. Tyler watched her go, knowing he'd hurt her by snapping at her.

She'd surprised him by showing up here. He hadn't wanted her to know that the man he was meeting with was the managing partner of a large law firm in St. Louis, here to interview Tyler for a job.

When Tyler had looked up and seen her, guilt had swept through him, and it had been his guilt that had made him cross with her.

He headed back to the table. He would apologize to Samantha later, explain to her how she'd thrown him by showing up here. Once he'd locked in a partnership at the St. Louis firm, he would sell her his half of Justice Inc. and they would both be better off in the long run.

Samantha had the cab take her directly home. She wasn't angry with Tyler. She wasn't even that hurt by his sharpness with her. It had been foolish and thoughtless of her to disturb his meeting. She could have waited

and talked to him later in the evening. As usual, she'd
allowed an impulse to rule her actions.

Once in the house, she decided to take a hot bath and
think again about the reports Wylie had given her.

Minutes later she was settled in the tub, her injured
leg propped out of the water and her head resting on an
inflatable pillow. The warm water soothed her, making
any thought nearly impossible.

She was half asleep when the phone rang. She
reached for the cordless near the tub. "Hello?"

"Samantha?" Tyler's voice drifted across the line.
"I just wanted to make sure you got home okay."

"I'm here." She sat up, realizing the water had
grown tepid.

"Samantha...I'm sorry I was so brusque with you at
the club."

"No, Tyler, I'm the one who should apologize for
interrupting your meeting. I found out a few things on
the Marcola case and wanted to bounce them off you.
I should have waited until you got back to the office.
In any case, we can talk when you get home."

"It will be a little while. I've got a few errands to
run."

"Where are you now?" she asked.

"At the airport. I had to drop somebody off."

"Would you mind stopping by the office and grabbing my briefcase off my desk?" she asked. Using her
toes, she managed to turn on the hot water faucet.

"No problem. What's that noise?"

"The hot water," she answered. "I'm in the bath-
tub." She smiled into the receiver. "If you hurry home,
Tyler, there will still be lots of bubbles."

"Samantha..."

"Hurry home, Tyler." She hung up and relaxed back

against the pillow. Tonight they would make love. And tonight she would tell him she loved him.

She shivered with excitement. If she was right about what she'd read in the reports, Dominic was on his way to an acquittal and hopefully Samantha was on the road to happiness with Tyler.

Tyler. Tonight she would tell him she loved him and he would confess that he loved her, too. Oh, he hadn't said the words to her yet, but she knew he did. His love shone in his eyes at unguarded moments, it showed in his worry about her health and more than anything, it radiated from him when they made love.

Moments later she got out of the tub and pulled on a loose lounging gown. It was Virginia's day off. Usually they ordered something in when Virginia wasn't there. Tonight she would surprise Tyler by cooking something. But first she wanted to make a phone call—follow up the lead that Wylie had provided.

She went to the phone in the kitchen and dialed Georgia Monroe's number. Omelettes…that was what she would make. Quick and easy, they were one of her few culinary specialties.

"Georgia, this is Samantha Dark," she said when the woman answered the phone. "I am so sorry to bother you, but I've managed to—uh—spill coffee over some of the notes I took the other day when I spoke to you," she improvised.

"Oh, honey, I do clumsy things like that all the time," Georgia replied with a friendly laugh.

"I was wondering if I could double-check some things with you…just for the record?"

"Of course. Whatever I can do to help."

"You said you saw Abigail when before the murder?"

"A couple of days before. Let me think...." Georgia paused thoughtfully. "Abigail was killed on a Wednesday and I guess it was Monday when I met her for lunch."

Samantha felt the flurry of excitement dance inside her. "And when did you tell me Kyle was born?"

A long pause followed. "I'm not sure what Kyle's birth date has to do with Abigail's death." A decided chill had replaced the friendliness in Georgia's voice.

"Neither do I," Samantha said. "But I'm wondering how it is you had a hysterectomy when you were thirty-five, then gave birth to Kyle when you were forty-two." She heard Georgia's soft gasp.

"You've done your homework well, Ms. Dark." There was another long pause. "Kyle was adopted, but I would prefer you wouldn't mention that fact to anyone. We decided not to tell Kyle. As far as he is concerned, as far as Morgan and I are concerned, he's ours."

"But I have a copy of his birth certificate here that shows Morgan as the father and you as the mother."

Again a pregnant pause filled the line. "Money can do miraculous things," Georgia finally answered.

"Thank you, Georgia, that's all I need from you for now." Samantha hung up the receiver and stared at it thoughtfully. So Kyle was adopted. Big deal. And Morgan and Georgia had obviously paid somebody off to hide the truth. How could that information help in Dominic's case?

She left the kitchen and went into the study, where the Marcola crime-scene photographs were spread across the top of her father's desk. Thankfully, the photographer had been zealous, as if he were being paid for each individual shot. There were pictures of Abigail on the bed, pictures of the champagne bottle and two glasses in the living room. Each and every room of the Monroe apartment had been captured on celluloid. Flipping through the more graphic ones, Samantha came to the photos of the kitchen.

"There," she said triumphantly as she stared at the picture that perfectly captured a foil-wrapped loaf of bread on the counter. A blue ribbon rode the center of the loaf. Blue for Wednesday. The day Abigail had died.

Georgia had lied. She'd seen Abigail at some point on the day of the young woman's murder. Why would Georgia lie unless she had something to hide?

Samantha went back to the kitchen and sank down at the table, suddenly chilled. Was it possible Abigail Monroe had somehow discovered the truth about Kyle and had threatened to tell the young man? Was it possible Georgia had killed Abigail in order to keep their secret safe? Samantha remembered the strength in the older woman's hands as she'd kneaded the bread dough. It was possible.

Where was Tyler? She needed to bounce these things off him, make sure she wasn't completely off track. Even if this hadn't been the motive for the murder, Samantha could use some of this information to cast reasonable doubt that Dominic was guilty.

She got up and began assembling the ingredients for the omelettes. As she chopped onions and green peppers, she tried to think of any other scenario that would make sense. As she diced ham and shredded cheese, she contemplated the strength of the information she'd gleaned.

She had no idea how long Tyler would be, so once she had everything ready to cook, she went back into the study and looked at the photos again. Even though she couldn't prove anything, would this information be enough to cast reasonable doubt? That was why she needed Tyler's input. She lacked the necessary objectivity.

She also scanned Wylie's report on Georgia again. She'd told Wylie she wanted to know everything there was to know about Morgan, Georgia and Kyle Monroe, and Rick Brennon. Wylie had been a genius, detailing their lives with information Samantha suspected he'd gained through both legal and illegal methods.

Georgia's hysterectomy had been done in a Kansas City hospital and Samantha suspected it had been performed there specifically so that nobody in Wilford would know about it. In the months preceding Kyle's birth, Georgia had been out of the country. Again, Samantha had a feeling she'd left so that nobody would know she wasn't pregnant. The adoption had probably been illegal, without proper paperwork or arrangements. But was that secret big enough to kill for?

Samantha raked a hand through her hair thoughtfully. She was savvy enough to know that sometimes it took a very small threat to drive a potential murderer over the edge.

She went to the window and looked out into approaching night. Where was Tyler? Surely he'd had enough time to run errands and get home. Where could he be?

Tyler had been offered a partnership in Bruner, Sandorf and Kearnes of St. Louis. Before seeing Leo Bruner off at the airport, Tyler had told the older man he would think about the offer. Bruner, Sandorf and Kearnes had a good reputation and was one of the powerhouse firms in the Midwest. Tyler knew he would be lucky to be a part of the business.

After running his errands, Tyler pulled into the parking space in front of Justice Inc. and for a moment simply sat in the car, staring at the building where he'd spent so much of his life for the past ten years.

Justice Inc. would never be the powerhouse that Bruner, Sandorf and Kearnes was. Jamison hadn't cared about expanding, bringing in more lawyers, more money. Justice Inc. had been his—and Tyler's. Tyler had put his heart and soul into the firm, making his work the single focus of his life.

He got out of the car and went inside. Instead of heading directly for Samantha's office, he went up to his own and sat down at his desk. Leaning back in his chair, he closed his eyes, his thoughts still a jumble of fear and regret, emotion and logic.

The idea of leaving Wilford and Justice Inc. caused an aching grief to pierce his soul, and yet he knew it was necessary. He couldn't remain here, working with Samantha, loving her yet remaining unwilling to take steps toward a permanent commitment to her. She deserved more than he could ever give.

But maybe he wouldn't have to leave, a small voice prodded hopefully. Samantha hadn't told him she loved him. Perhaps he was making a mountain out of a molehill. Maybe she really was just having fun, experimenting with her first sexual relationship. Eventually the novelty would wear off and she would seek a more permanent, life partner.

He had no idea how long he sat there, lost in thought, when he heard the first faint noise that told him he wasn't alone in the building. He leaned forward, straining to hear, wondering if it had just been the clang of the heat ducts or something more ominous.

A new noise, the furtive slap of feet against a floor, made his stomach tighten in response. Had he sat here so long that Samantha had grown tired of waiting and come to retrieve her briefcase herself?

He left his office and went to the top of the stairs and looked down. A faint light spilled from the doorway of Samantha's office. Apprehension turned to irritation. She was the most impatient, irksome woman he'd ever known. He could hear the shuffle of papers from where he stood.

"Samantha, I told you I'd get your briefcase for you," he said as he came down the stairs. The sounds ceased and once again Tyler felt a whisper of anxiety sweep through him.

Samantha would have answered him. She would have had a smart-mouth reply. Tyler paused midway on the stairs, unsure whether to go forward or back.

The silence stretched taut. Tyler imagined he could hear the sound of the person's breathing, then realized it was his own. Cautiously, he stepped down a stair, then another and another until he was on the ground floor just outside Samantha's office door.

Drawing a deep breath, his adrenaline pumping like fire in his blood, he whirled into the office. Nobody. A glowing ring of light from the desk lamp surrounded the desk. Tyler frowned. Had he only imagined the noises?

When he saw the files spilling out of the cabinet and

the papers strewn around the floor, he knew he hadn't imagined anything. Somebody had been here. Somebody other than Samantha.

Hearing a sound behind him, he spun around. "You!" Tyler gasped in surprise, just as Jamison's favorite pewter statue came down on his head.

Chapter 13

Samantha looked at the clock for the hundredth time in the past hour, wondering what could be keeping Tyler. When the doorbell rang, she jumped up from the desk, certain it must be him and he'd forgotten his key.

She pulled open the door, surprised to see Bones standing on the porch. "Bones! What's going on? What are you doing here?"

"I've got some information for you, Samantha. Stuff that might help your client."

"Come in." She gestured him into the hallway, then pointed to the study doorway. "Let's go in there and we can talk."

"Hey, nice place," Bones said as he stepped into the study. He walked over to the bar, eyeing the bottles. "Do you mind?"

"Help yourself." She sat in one of the wing chairs and waited impatiently for him to help himself to a healthy shot of Tyler's favorite brandy. "So, what have you got for me?'' she asked once he'd seated himself in the chair opposite hers.

He took a sip of brandy and leaned back in the chair with a contented sigh. ''Ah, this is the life. I can't believe you left all this behind when you left Wilford.''

''There's more to life than a big house,'' Samantha returned, patience wearing thin. ''So, what do you have to tell me, Bones? I've got precious little time to figure out how to save Dominic from a conviction.''

''Did I ever tell you I used to do a little gardening?''

Samantha stared at the tall, thin man, wondering what on earth he was talking about. ''That's nice, Bones, but—''

''Yeah, worked for Georgia Monroe for a couple of years. Sweet lady, Georgia. I was there when Morgan told her he wanted a divorce.'' He shook his head, his eyes glittering as they focused on Samantha. ''Sad. The poor woman was devastated. After all she'd done for him. She took in his illegitimate child, raised him as her own, and that's the thanks she got.''

Samantha tensed. ''I had no idea you and Georgia were so close.''

''Georgia could live with the divorce,'' Bones continued. ''At least she had her dignity left, but then Abigail found out about Kyle, and threatened to tell everyone. Everyone in town would know that Morgan not only divorced her, but had cheated on her throughout their marriage. Georgia couldn't live with that. She'd be the butt of bad jokes around town. And so she called me and we talked about what a problem Abigail had become.''

Fear slithered up Samantha's spine as she gazed at the man she'd trusted, had thought was her friend. She felt as if she were caught in a spider web, held prisoner by Bones's gaze, the matter-of-fact tone of his voice. She knew she should do something…that she was in danger, but she couldn't move. "How…"

Bones smiled and set his brandy glass down by the foot of his chair. "The how was easy. Georgia paid a little visit to Abigail that morning, spiked the bottle of champagne with a handful of her sleeping pills. She knew Abigail loved her champagne, drank it every evening."

"Dominic?"

"Wasn't supposed to be there." Bones grinned. "Imagine my surprise when I opened that bedroom door and found not one, but two unconscious people on the bed." He shrugged. "Dominic was an unexpected gift. I knew if I let him live, he'd probably go down as the murderer and the case would be closed." He frowned and rubbed his forehead. "But you wouldn't leave it alone. You had to dig and dig." He eyed Samantha with a touch of sympathy. "I tried to scare you off, Samantha. First with the brick, then with that." He pointed to the cast on her leg.

At that moment, whatever spell had held her motionless in the chair snapped. He'd broken her leg. She drew in a deep breath, aware that she couldn't function on impulse, had to remain calm and rational. Bones was dangerous, and the fact that he'd confessed to killing Abigail meant he didn't intend for Samantha to live to use that information against him.

"It was easy to get Rick Brennon's money clip. Most nights he gets drunk and leaves it lying on top of the bar. I left it next to you to muddy the waters. I didn't want to hurt you, Samantha. Why couldn't you just leave it all alone?"

"Because an innocent man was going to prison," she

retorted. "You'd better get out of here, Bones. Tyler should be home any minute. If you go now, perhaps you can escape, leave town."

Bones gave her a sly, ugly smile that walked cold fingers of dread up Samantha's spine. "Tyler won't be joining you this evening—or any other evening, for that matter."

Samantha's breath caught painfully in her chest. "Wha—what does that mean?"

"Tyler met with a horrible accident at the law firm. A statue fell on his head."

Samantha felt the world shift beneath her. For a single moment her heart seemed to stop beating as she tried to imagine this world without Tyler in it. No, no, it couldn't be so! her heart cried. Not now, when she'd finally discovered the depth of her love for him.

The thought of Bones hurting Tyler filled her with an uncontrollable rage. Without hesitating, she thrust herself out of her chair and swung her broken leg up in the air, the heavy cast catching him full on the side of the head. With a grunt of surprise and pain, Bones toppled out of his chair and to the floor.

Samantha didn't hang around to see what damage she'd done. She ran, her cast bumping clumsily against the carpet. Behind her she heard a cry of rage, a threat of death. She hurried in the only direction she could—up the stairs.

Tyler came to with a groan. The first thing he saw when he opened his eyes was Jamison's pewter statue of Justice, her eyes blindfolded, the scales she held covered with blood. Blood? Why was the statue bloody? Confusion swirled in his brain.

He sat up, for a moment disoriented as he looked

around the office. The left side of his head pounded with a nauseating intensity. He touched it and was surprised when his fingers came away bloody. He stared at the statue—his blood.

With a gasp, he remembered. He stood, shoving away the dizziness that tried to grip him. Samantha. Her name raced through him with a prayer. Dear God, how long had he been knocked out? He had no idea why Bones had been in the office or what he'd been after, but as Tyler thought of Samantha alone in the house, his blood ran cold with heart-stopping fear.

He had to get to her, tell her Bones couldn't be trusted. As he raced out of the building, his head ached not only from the physical blow it had sustained, but also from the confusion and questions that ripped through it.

Why had Bones been skulking around in Samantha's office? What could he have to do with anything? Nothing made sense. Nothing except Tyler's driving need to get to Samantha.

He suspected that Bones had assumed the blow to Tyler's head had been a lethal one. Thank God for his excellent reflexes, Tyler thought. He'd managed to jerk his head in the instant before the statue made contact, transforming a killer blow into little more than a glancing one.

Still the questions came. What in the hell had Bones been after? What was so important he would kill for it? Did all this have something to do with Abigail Monroe's death? Had he left Tyler lying on the office floor and gone to harm Samantha?

Tyler's heart felt as if it would burst from his chest as he sped down Main Street toward the Dark mansion. Please...please... The words were a prayer, a litany against evil. It couldn't happen again. He had to reach Samantha in time.

He felt as if one of his nightmares had surrounded him, was overwhelming him. He remembered the sight of the police cars, the flashing lights—the sight of his mother dead. If only he'd gone home on time. If only he hadn't blown off his curfew, he might have gotten home in time to save her. His fault…his fault…

He had to get home, had to save Samantha. He should have gone into her office, grabbed the briefcase, and headed home instead of sitting for so long at his desk.

It was all his fault—just like it had been when he was fourteen. If anything happened to Samantha he would go mad. He had to get to her in time.

As he turned down the long winding driveway that led to the house, his heart thundered with fear. Although there were no police cars, nothing to indicate a scene from his nightmares, he knew with certainty that Bones had come here for Samantha. Oh, God, don't let him be too late.

The car squealed to a halt and Tyler was out and running before the motor had stopped. He exploded through the front door. "Samantha?" His cry was immediately swallowed by the utter silence of the house.

He strode into the study, his heart banging harshly against his chest. An overturned chair…a broken glass…a picture askew. Something bad had happened in here. His stomach ached, rivaling the pain in his head.

"Samantha!" He bellowed her name. He didn't care about Bones hearing him. If Bones was still here, he wouldn't catch Tyler unaware again. And Tyler would kill him if he'd harmed Samantha. He would kill him

with a rage that had been bottled up for years, the rage
that now bubbled inside him.

It took him only a moment to search the ground floor.
Samantha was nowhere to be found. The side of his
head hurt with the piercing intensity of a toothache, but
he ignored the pain. Nothing mattered except finding
Samantha.

He stood at the bottom of the staircase and looked
up. The hallway was shadowy, although lights spilled
out from each bedroom. He knew he wasn't alone in
the house, knew it the way an animal could sense the
presence of its prey.

He dreaded climbing the stairs, afraid he would enter
one of the rooms to find Samantha on one of the
beds—dead. Just as his mother had been. He couldn't
survive it again. He would go mad with pain. With guilt.

He climbed the stairs slowly, dreading what he might
find, warily listening for sounds that would indicate he
wasn't alone.

When he got to the top of the stairs he paused, still
listening intently. Rational thought fell away as survival
instincts kicked in. He kept any thought of Samantha
out of his mind, knowing that to dwell on the possibility
of her death would render him incapacitated.

He moved to the first bedroom door, wishing for a
gun…a knife…anything that could be used as a weapon
against Bones. His only comfort was his guess that
Bones had no real weapon, either. Had Bones had a gun
or a knife, he would have used them on Tyler at the
office.

The first bedroom was empty. Tyler leaned against
the wall and took a steadying breath. Where was Samantha? Her bedroom was empty as well. As was Tyler's. In each room the closet doors hung open, as if

somebody had looked inside, seeking something—or someone.

Tyler methodically worked his way down the hall until he stood in front of the closed door that led to Samantha's mother's room. If anyone was in the house, they had to be in this room. He gripped the doorknob, his palm slick with sweat. It made no noise as it turned and the door opened.

He released a sigh as he saw that the room was empty. Samantha wasn't dead on the bed, nor did anyone else appear to be anywhere in the room. So, where was she?

A chilling wind swept through him. Had Bones come here and taken her someplace else? At this very moment was she locked in a car trunk? Being driven to the place where she would be murdered?

He started to leave the room, but hesitated as he saw the edge of the curtain caught in the closed balcony door. Frozen with fear, he stared at the door. Oh, God. No.

On wooden legs, he walked to the door, afraid to look out...afraid he would find Samantha below the balcony, broken in pieces on the patio below. He yanked open the door and gasped.

Samantha was there. With Bones. He had her pulled up against him, a knife held to her neck as she stood precariously close to the broken railing. A knife. Dammit. Tyler had hoped Bones would be weaponless, that the fight would be even.

"Stay back or I'll slice her and throw her over the edge," Bones threatened.

Samantha's eyes were black with fear. "He killed Abigail, Tyler. And he's the son of a bitch who broke my leg."

In some disjointed part of his brain, Tyler realized it wasn't fear darkening her eyes; it was pure, undiluted anger.

"What do you want?" Tyler demanded as he weighed his options. He couldn't rush the man. The balcony was too small for such action. He would either fly over the edge or Bones would do as he'd warned and either slash Samantha's throat or throw her over. It was too risky.

"I just want to get out of here. Things have fallen apart. Now, back up."

"Let her go," Tyler demanded.

Bones shook his head, his arm tightening around Samantha's neck. "She's my insurance. She comes with me. When I'm in a safe place I'll let her go."

Tyler knew the man was lying. He and Samantha knew too much for Bones to let them survive this night. Still, fearing Bones might follow up on his threat, Tyler backed up into the bedroom. At least in here, he would have space to maneuver.

As Tyler backed into the room, Bones and Samantha advanced. Tyler tensed, readying himself to attack.

"Don't even think about it," Bones warned as if reading his mind. "I can slice and dice her before you ever get to me." As if to prove his point, he touched the tip of the knife to Samantha's neck. She gasped a cry of pain as a tiny rivulet of blood bubbled from the tiny wound. Tyler felt the swirling darkness of his deepest rage.

"If you hurt her again, I'll kill you." Tyler's voice sounded distant to his ears, filled with the cold, murderous instinct he'd once felt as a young man. He wouldn't have it twice in a lifetime—not the death of somebody he loved. He would die himself before he would allow Bones to hurt Samantha.

Bones laughed with a chilling sound. "I'd say you're in no position to threaten me." His eyes narrowed. "Now, back out of the room and head downstairs."

Unable to do anything else, Tyler did as he was told. As he backed down the stairs, his mind raced, seeking a way out that wouldn't get Samantha killed in the process.

He reached the foyer and stared up to where Bones and Samantha slowly made their way down the stairs, the knife never wavering from beneath Samantha's chin.

God help him, he didn't know what to do, didn't know how to save her. The knife point pressed into the soft flesh of Samantha's throat made any rescue attempt impossible.

Tyler clenched and unclenched his hand in futility. Helpless. He was utterly helpless and he knew if Bones harmed Samantha he'd kill Bones...but if anything happened to Samantha, Tyler also realized something would die inside him.

Halfway down the stairs, Samantha realized she had to do something. Bones wouldn't be satisfied with just killing her. When he finished her he would go after Tyler. Tyler was strong, and she saw the rage that filled him, but his strength and anger couldn't compete with a slashing knife. She couldn't allow Bones to get to Tyler. She had to do something—fast.

Each step they took was awkward, hampered by Samantha's cast and their dual movements as Bones tried to keep her close to him. Drawing a deep breath, knowing she might spend the rest of her life in a body cast, in one swift motion, Samantha smacked Bones's hand that held the knife. As it clattered down the stairs, Samantha willed herself limp.

"Hey!"

Vaguely aware of Bones's startled cry, she slid out of his grasp and tumbled head over heels down the stairs. She felt the brunt of each step against her body—bruising...pounding—until she hit the foyer on her back, her cast smacking against the floor with a dull thud.

"Samantha!" Tyler cried, and crouched over her as Bones turned and ran back up the stairs.

"Don't just stand there...go after him," she managed to gasp.

After only a moment's hesitation, Tyler thundered up the stairs after Bones.

Cautiously, Samantha sat up, checking for the pain that would indicate something broken. Although sore, she didn't think the fall had caused any major damage. She stood and picked up the knife, then lumbered up the stairs to help Tyler.

She found the two men back in her mother's bedroom, brawling like two drunks in a bar. She stood in the doorway, unsure what to do as Tyler and Bones threw punches that landed on each other with deadly accuracy.

The side of Tyler's head was bloodied and one of his eyes was swelling. Bones's bottom lip had split and was leaking blood that smeared across his chin.

The men appeared evenly matched—Tyler with his anger and Bones with the need to survive. Back and forth their punches flew, like two boxers fighting to the finish.

Samantha screamed as they locked together and barreled out of the room and onto the balcony. She raced to the door, terror sweeping through her as their struggle brought them dangerously close to the edge.

She wanted to give Tyler the knife, but was afraid that somehow it would end up back in Bones's hands. The two rolled on the balcony floor, first Bones on top of Tyler, then Tyler on top of Bones. Neither seemed to be able to get the upper hand.

Closer and closer to the brink they rolled, until finally Bones was on top of Tyler, Tyler's torso hanging over the edge, through the space where her father had fallen, below the single board intended as a barrier. As Tyler's hands sought purchase, gripping the lip of the balcony floor, Bones slid off him and began to shove him.

With a scream of outrage, Samantha attacked, plunging the knife deep into Bones's back. He stiffened as the knife sank in, his face displaying shock. He stood, wavering like a reed in the wind, then fell over the edge and to the concrete below.

Sobbing, Samantha helped Tyler to safety. He stood and immediately wrapped her in his embrace. "I killed him," she cried.

Tyler hugged her tighter. "No, you saved me." He kissed her forehead, her tearstained cheeks, then her lips.

She clung to him, wondering if she would ever forget the moment when she thought he would plunge to his death. "I was so afraid," she sobbed.

"It's over now," he said softly. "It's all over."

He led her back into the house and down the stairs. He called the police, then they sat in the study to await the arrival of the authorities.

"It was Georgia. She's responsible for Abigail's death." Samantha told Tyler what she'd learned from the reports Wylie had given her. "She sent Bones here after I called her. She knew that I knew about the adoption." Samantha shivered. "I think it was a combination of things that pushed her over the edge—the divorce, Morgan's marriage to Abigail, then Abigail threatening to tell about Kyle's parentage. She hired Bones to kill Abigail. Dominic just happened to be in the wrong place at the wrong time."

Tyler held her close and she squeezed her eyes closed, remembering those moments before Tyler had arrived, when Bones had bragged about the murder, about breaking her leg in order to scare her off the case. He'd intended to kill her on the balcony. Would have killed her if Tyler hadn't arrived when he had.

"The important thing is you did what you wanted to do. Dominic will be released."

Yes, Dominic was vindicated. She'd been right all along. She smiled up at Tyler. "I'm one hell of a lawyer, aren't I?"

He returned her smile. "You're not just one hell of a lawyer—you're one hell of a woman."

Before he could say anything more, the sound of sirens filled the room and there was knocking at the door. The police had arrived.

"Tired?" Tyler closed the front door after the last officer had left. Dawn streaked strands of brilliant orange across the eastern sky. It had been a night of questions and explanations.

Samantha nodded. "Exhausted."

"Why don't you go to bed? There's nothing more that needs to be done. Dominic will be released. Georgia is under arrest and from what the sheriff told me, she has made a full confession." Georgia had spilled her guts, telling the police of her hatred for Abigail, who'd stolen her husband and intended to wreak havoc on her life by exposing the secret that Kyle was Morgan's, but not hers. The secret Abigail had been killed for was that Kyle was the result of an illicit affair. And Georgia hadn't wanted the good people of Wilford to know her husband had been unfaithful to her during their marriage. She'd killed Abigail for pride.

"There's one more thing I need to take care of before I can rest," Samantha said. She thrust her hand into the pocket of her gown and withdrew an earring.

"I don't understand." Tyler looked at her curiously. He wasn't sure who looked worse, her or him. His left eye was nearly swollen shut and he felt as if he'd been through a meat grinder. Samantha looked little better. Blood splattered the front of her gown and her face was devoid of color.

"When Bones was after me, I hid on the balcony, hoping he wouldn't find me and would eventually go away. While I was hiding there, I found this between the cracks of the floorboards." She held the earring up between her fingers. Large, and shaped like a four-leaf clover with a tiny emerald in the center, it sparkled in the foyer light.

"I recognized it," she said. "When I was seventeen, I bought these earrings for Edie's birthday." Her gaze captured his intently. "I need to talk to Edie. I need to find out how and when this got on the balcony."

"Samantha…" He began a protest, but saw the resolve in her eyes and knew she wouldn't let it rest until she had her answers. "Okay. We go to Edie's," he said in resignation. "Although we might want to clean up a bit first."

It was a little over an hour later when they got into

the car and Tyler headed toward Edie's apartment building on the other side of town.

"How's your head?" Samantha broke into his thoughts.

"A little sore, but the paramedics assured me it was nothing to worry about." Samantha had insisted his wounds be looked at by the paramedics who had shown up with the police.

"I knew there was nothing to worry about. You're too hardheaded for a little statue to do much damage." She flashed him a smile and his love for her welled up in his throat, making it impossible for him to reply.

The Marcola case was over. Dominic was free. Tyler knew he would have to tell her he was leaving, accepting the offer with the firm in St. Louis. But now wasn't the time. Later. He would tell her later.

He cast her a surreptitious glance. She looked beyond exhaustion. Dark smudges had appeared beneath her eyes and she grimaced as she changed positions. "Are you sure you're up to this? We could always talk to Edie later."

She shook her head. "No. I need to do this now." She looked down at the earring she held in her hand. "This earring on the balcony doesn't make sense. Father's fall from the balcony doesn't make sense. I need to do this now."

"There could be a reasonable explanation for the earring," he replied.

She looked at him, her features revealing a weariness that tugged at his heart. "I hope there is," she whispered.

Tyler parked in front of the large brick building where Edie had her apartment on the third floor. "You want me to wait here?" he asked.

"No. I want you with me." She reached out and took his hand in hers. "I know you think I'm half crazy and I'm sure this is all a wild-goose chase. But I owe it to my father to make sure. I know he wouldn't jump off the balcony, and I can't imagine him falling accidentally." She squeezed Tyler's hand. "I feel like so much of my life has been filled with loose ends. I owe it to myself to follow this through, so Father's death doesn't haunt me forever."

Tyler nodded. He reached out and touched the tiny wound Bones's knife had left in her neck. It would heal. Leaving Samantha would leave behind a wound, but he hoped it would eventually heal, as well. She was one hell of a woman and she deserved one hell of a man. Unfortunately, Tyler knew he could never be that man.

Chapter 14

"Samantha...Tyler..."

Edie greeted them at the door, clad in a housecoat and slippers. Her features registered her surprise as she looked at first one, then the other. "What's going on? Has something happened? Tyler...your eye." She placed her hands on her hips. "Would somebody please tell me what's happened?" she demanded.

"Can we come in?" Samantha asked, the cold early-morning air slicing through her. She knew if what she suspected was true, this was going to be difficult, and she wanted it over and done with as soon as possible.

"Of course." Edie opened the door wider to allow them inside. "Come on into the kitchen."

They followed her through a tidy living room, into a small but cheerful kitchen. "Sit." She gestured them toward chairs at the round oak table. "I'll pour coffee for us all. You both look like you could use a cup. Or a pot," she added dryly.

As Edie poured the coffee, Samantha filled her in on the latest in the Marcola case and the events that had occurred with Bones the night before.

"I can't believe it, although Georgia Monroe was always much too proud, too concerned with what people thought of her, but I never dreamed she'd go to such lengths," Edie said when Samantha had finished telling her all the news. "You're both lucky to be alive."

She rocked back in her chair and gazed at Samantha fondly. "So, your client goes free. You've done your job well." She shook her head, a wistful, almost-haunted smile on her face. "Your father would have been so proud of you. He was thrilled enough when he learned you were going to law school."

Samantha stared at Edie in surprise. "What do you mean? How could he have known about that? I didn't tell anyone when I started law school."

"Wylie didn't tell you?"

"Wylie? Tell me what?" Samantha's heart thundered in anticipation.

"One of the last jobs Wylie did for your daddy was to check up on you and make sure you were all right," Edie said. "Your father was brokenhearted when you ran away, but he was always aware of where you were and what you were doing, ready to step in if you needed him."

"Wylie never mentioned it," Samantha replied, her heart seeming to lodge in her throat. She had been important to him. He had cared about her.

"He wouldn't have," Tyler observed. "Wylie wouldn't break Jamison's confidence."

"Jamison was proud that you had the strength, the guts to take off and build a life for yourself. He told me once that you were doing it just like he had—on your own, using your brains and determination.'' Edie reached across the table and patted Samantha's hand. ''And he would have burst his buttons with pride over this. You not only got your client off, you solved the whole damn case.''

Samantha extracted her hand from Edie's. ''And now I need your help in solving another case.''

Edie frowned. ''What? You know I'll do whatever I can to help you.''

Samantha withdrew the earring from her coat pocket and held it up for Edie to view. ''Does this look familiar?''

Edie gasped. ''My earring!'' She reached out and took the piece of jewelry from Samantha. ''I wondered what had happened to it. I remember when you gave these to me.''

''Aren't you going to ask me where I found it?''

''Of course,'' Edie answered quickly. ''Where did you find it?''

''On the balcony where Father fell.'' Samantha paused for a moment as Edie averted her gaze and stared down at the earring in her hand. ''Edie, the man you mentioned to me…the man you were in love with…it was my father, wasn't it?''

Edie didn't answer, nor did she raise her gaze to look at Samantha. ''I don't know what you're talking about,'' she finally said, her voice a mere whisper.

''You never could lie worth a damn, Edie,'' Samantha replied tersely. ''Edie, I don't want to hurt you,'' she said more gently. ''I just want to know the truth. How did your earring get on the balcony? I need to know what happened. Please.''

Edie appeared to crumble before Samantha's eyes. Her plump shoulders slumped forward and tears trekked down her cheeks, splashing onto the front of her brightly colored housecoat. When she finally raised her head and looked at Samantha, her eyes radiated a tortured pain that stole Samantha's breath away.

"Yes, I loved Jamison," she finally gulped out amid her tears. "I think I fell in love with him the first day he interviewed me for the job. But nothing happened between us until you were about twelve. That's when we started seeing each other on a personal level. We became lovers."

Samantha sat back in her chair, surprised, yet somehow not surprised. She'd never given much thought to her father's private life—the fact that he was a man and might need a woman. Edie was the logical choice. She'd been available, both emotionally and physically.

Samantha's head filled with tiny pieces of memories. Edie's intimate knowledge of their house and her father. Edie's presence at birthday parties and the occasional family gathering.

The clues had been there, but Samantha had been too embroiled in her own unhappiness, the angst of her own life, to see what was going on around her. "So what happened?" she finally asked.

Edie swiped at her tearstained cheeks and smiled bitterly. "What happened? Nothing happened. He came here or I'd go to the house. We'd sleep together, then I'd go home or he'd go home." She got up and grabbed a handful of tissues from a decorated box on the counter, then sat down once again.

"At first, I didn't mind. Whatever piece of himself Jamison wanted to give, I eagerly took. But in my heart, I dreamed that eventually we'd get married. I loved you and Melissa, dreamed of the four of us being a family. As the years passed and nothing changed, I tried to be

patient. I knew he mourned for your mother, but I
thought eventually that would pass. Dear God, how long
could a man mourn?'' She laughed bitterly.

Tyler reached for Samantha's hand, as if knowing
whatever Edie said next would be difficult to hear. Samantha squeezed his hand tightly, although inside she
was curiously numb. ''What happened that night on the
balcony? How did Father fall?'' she asked softly.

Edie stared at the tissues in her hand as she methodically pulled them into tiny pieces. ''Jamison called me
about seven to come to the house. Tyler was gone and
it was Virginia's night off. As usual, I got there and
we...we slept together.'' Her cheeks flamed red and
tears once again filled her eyes. ''When—when we were
finished, we talked for a little while, then as usual he
told me I could go on home. This time it made me mad.
I felt cheap and I told him so. I told him I was tired of
being his little secret, that I'd given him years of my
life and it was time he made a commitment. He
laughed.''

She looked at Samantha beseechingly. ''Sometimes
your daddy could be cruel.''

Samantha nodded, her heart aching for Edie's pain
and for remnants of her own childhood pains. She could
envision Edie's heartbreak—needing, wanting to belong
to something bigger than herself; giving her heart and
soul to a man, only to have him deal her the ultimate
rejection.

''Anyway—'' Edie sniffed and dabbed at her eyes
''—he told me he cared about me, but he was satisfied
with our relationship, that he'd never marry me. We
argued. He left the room and went into your mother's
bedroom and I followed him there. I was so angry, so
hurt. I kept hammering at him, telling him he had to let

go of her. She was gone and wasn't coming back."
Edie's words came faster and faster, spilling from her
without breath. "I pulled him out on the balcony to
show him the place where she'd fallen. I—I didn't mean
for it to happen.... He—he said more hateful things and
I just shoved at him, wanting him to stop talking. He
was too close to the edge—off balance—and he fell."
Edie's voice rose hysterically, then she dissolved in
sobs.

Now she knew. Despite the circumstances, a sense of
strange peace swept through Samantha. All the pieces
were now in their proper place. She could let it go now.

"I didn't mean to...." Edie buried her head on the
table. "I loved him. Oh, God, I loved him so much. I
just wanted him to forget her. To love me..."

Samantha stood and motioned Tyler toward the door.
There was nothing left to learn here, nothing left to do.
It was time to go home.

"You going to call the sheriff?" Tyler asked, moments later when they were back in his car and heading
home.

Samantha shook her head. "What's the point? I believe Edie. It was just like the authorities ruled it—a
tragic accident."

"You could probably have her brought up on charges
of manslaughter."

"To what end?" She looked out the window.
"There's been enough tragedy, enough pain. It's time
to move on. Edie will have to live with her memories
of that horrible night. That's more than enough punish-
ment."

For a few moments they rode in silence. Samantha
continued to stare out the window, trying to make sense

of all that had happened, all she had learned in the last twenty-four hours.

Exhaustion tugged at her, weighing her down. Her body ached from her fall down the stairs. Her eyes felt grainy, her heart almost numb. Still, she sought reasons for all that had happened, for logic in a world gone mad. "I keep thinking there's something to be learned from all this...but I'm just too tired to figure it all out," she finally said.

"The lesson is that loving somebody can be hazardous," Tyler replied.

Samantha turned and looked at him in surprise. "Surely you don't really believe that."

He shrugged, his features reflecting his own brand of exhaustion. "Think about it. Abigail Monroe died because Georgia loved Morgan and Kyle too much. Dominic was arrested because everyone knew he loved Abigail. Your father died because Edie loved him, because he loved your mother too much. It's not exactly a testimony for the wonders of love." He pulled into the Dark driveway and parked.

"You're wrong...." She forced a smile. "But I'm too tired to figure out how you're wrong. Later. Later we'll argue about this."

Together they got out of the car and went into the house. Samantha eyed the staircase tiredly. With the cast on her leg, going up the stairs required maximum energy.

"Let me help," Tyler offered, and scooped her up in his arms.

Gratefully, she relaxed in his embrace and placed her head against his chest, loving the steady sound of his heartbeat.

She suddenly remembered all the plans she'd made

for the night before. The omelettes she'd been going to cook, a night of making love, her intention to finally tell Tyler she loved him.

Now certainly didn't seem like the right time. They were both too tired, too overloaded for proclamations of love. Later. She closed her eyes as he carried her up the stairs and to her bedroom. She didn't open them until he gently placed her on her bed. Then she grabbed his hand. "Stay here with me," she said softly, sleepily. She wanted to sleep knowing he was right next to her.

"Samantha...I..."

"Please, Tyler. Sleep beside me. I just want to know you're here."

He hesitated for a moment, then nodded. He took off her shoes, then kicked off his own and stretched out beside her. Within minutes, she slept.

Tyler watched her sleep. His own exhaustion tugged at him but he fought against it, knowing this would be the last time he saw Samantha this intimately.

Never again would he allow himself the pleasure of watching her sleep, of holding her in his arms, of loving her. Eventually, with time and distance, he hoped he would forget the sweet scent of her hair, the richness of her laughter, her quick mind that stimulated, provoked and endeared. With enough time he would forget the spark in her eyes, the curve of her lips, the warmth of her body pressed against his. Eventually he would forget he'd ever loved her at all.

He rolled over on his back and stared at the ceiling, his thoughts flying over all the events that had taken place in the last hours.

He'd suspected for a long time that Jamison had been seeing a woman. His mentor would disappear sometimes in the evenings for a couple of hours—although he certainly hadn't suspected Edie. Sad. It was all so sad. There never seemed to be any winners in the game of love.

There had been a time when Tyler had wanted to emulate everything about Jamison; had admired his strength, his power, even his coldness of character. He wasn't sure he wanted that anymore. He was no longer sure what he wanted.

He rolled over and looked at Samantha once again. At least she had found her peace. She and Melissa were on the road to a new, close relationship and she knew now that despite her father's lack of affection, he had loved his daughters. She would have Justice Inc. to keep her busy. With the triumph of the Marcola case behind her, she would probably have more work than she would know what to do with.

Eventually, she would meet another man, one who was capable of loving her as she loved—wholly, without constraint, without fear. Yes, Samantha would be fine. And he would do what he always did—somehow survive. He closed his eyes and within minutes was asleep.

He awoke several hours later, the sun streaming full into the bedroom window. He stretched, feeling surprisingly rested, then turned over to look at Samantha. Her half of the bed was empty, the pillow still holding the imprint of her head.

"Samantha?" he called as he sat up. There was no reply.

He went into the bathroom and sluiced cold water on his face, ridding himself of the last remnants of sleep. His eye was still swollen and red, although less sore than it had been.

"Samantha?" he called again as he went downstairs. She was not in the study, nor in the kitchen. He looked in the garage and realized her car was gone. Instantly he knew where she was.

He grabbed his coat and headed for his car. He drove to the cemetery where Abigail Monroe had been buried—and where Jamison Dark had been laid to rest. He'd had a feeling he would find Samantha here...finally able to say her goodbyes to her father.

He parked his car next to hers and got out. In the distance he could see her, at her father's grave.

The fact that he'd known instinctively she would come here made him realize how deep their relationship had grown. There had been a time when he wouldn't have hazarded a guess at where she might go or what she might do. Now his heart knew hers.

His footsteps were soundless as he made his way toward her.

She didn't appear to hear his approach above the moan of the wintry wind. He stopped when he got to about ten feet behind her, not wanting to intrude on her private time, but wanting to be here in case she needed him.

Crouched down, she clutched a bouquet of bright yellow mums, their color vivid against the browns and grays that surrounded them. The hand holding the bouquet trembled slightly, whether from the cold or from emotion, Tyler couldn't be sure.

"Oh, Daddy, I'm sorry for expecting too much from you."

Her voice carried to where Tyler stood, riding the wind with sorrow. He heard the tears she suppressed, wanted to run to her, hold her, but knew she needed to grieve—finally.

"I realize now you loved me in the only way you could...." She lowered her head, her next words muffled. "Sorry...love you..." Bits and pieces of her one-sided conversation fluttered to Tyler's ears. A daughter's regrets...and a daughter's forgiveness. He heard the sound of her tears, but knew they were healthy ones, cathartic and healing.

He turned to leave, realizing she wouldn't need him. She'd made her final peace with her childhood; had grown up enough to understand the frailty of parenting, the imperfections of humans.

"Love Tyler..."

He stopped, frozen in his tracks as these words filtered to him, through him. Unable to help himself, he took a step closer, not wanting to hear anything further, yet incapable of moving away.

"I love him as I've never loved anyone before...like you must have loved Mama." The tears were gone, replaced with a vibrancy and joy that tore through Tyler. No, please, don't love me, his heart cried.

He watched as she touched Jamison's headstone, with a loving, caressing gesture. "He makes me happy, Daddy. And we're going to get married and fill that house with your grandchildren."

Tyler's throat closed up and he felt as if he were suffocating. The wind stung his eyes, bringing tears. He hadn't wanted to hear those words. He hadn't wanted to believe that she could love him.

He pressed a hand against his stomach, where it burned and ached, then realized the pain was higher—surrounding his heart.

Dammit, he hadn't wanted to hear her say the words. It made her love for him real—and his for her impossible. It made his leaving so much more difficult. And he *had* to leave. Without making a sound, Tyler turned and walked back to his car.

Samantha had said all she needed to say, yet she was reluctant to leave. Although the wind was cold, the warmth of her heart banished any chill.

Her memories of growing up with her father would always sadden her, but now those memories of his seeming distance, his coolness, were tempered with understanding. And with understanding came forgiveness.

He *had* loved her. It hadn't been a perfect love, but it had been all he'd had to give. He'd even hired Wylie Brooks to make certain she was all right. And if she had any lingering doubts of his love, all she had to do was remind herself that he'd left to her half of what he'd loved most dearly—Justice Inc.

He'd bequeathed her half of his life's work, and a partner she'd managed to fall in love with. Void of the anger and hurt that had driven her for so long, she felt free and cleansed, eager to open her heart to Tyler.

She now realized the lesson to be learned from the events of the past several days. Heart at peace, she touched her father's headstone one last time. "Goodbye, Daddy. I love you." She placed the flowers at the foot of the gravestone, then turned and hurried for her car, eager to talk to Tyler…eager to share her love.

Chapter 15

Tyler wasn't home when Samantha returned. She had no idea where he might have gone, but wasn't worried about his absence. It was just after noon and it was possible he'd gone to the office to take care of some business. She knew that his involvement in the Marcola case had caused him to neglect some of his own pending cases.

Samantha busied herself putting away the omelette makings she'd prepared, then never cooked the night before. Virginia had arrived early that morning while Tyler and Samantha had been cleaning up to go to Edie's, and Samantha had sent the older woman home for the day.

As Samantha tidied the kitchen, she was glad she'd sent Virginia away. The simple, mundane task of washing dishes and countertops felt good. It was just the kind of mindless work she needed while she mentally prepared for spilling her heart to Tyler.

She smiled as she thought of him. Who would have thought those ice blue eyes of his would be the ones she wanted to look into for the rest of her life? Who could have imagined that his wry sense of humor, his highly moral convictions would send a shiver of excitement up and down her spine?

Although she knew their differences in philosophy and the way they approached life would continue to cause contention between them, she was confident they had enough love for each other to survive living together, building a life together.

Although Tyler hadn't actually told her he loved her, she knew he did. Perhaps he didn't even realize it yet, but he loved her as deeply, as passionately as she loved him. "And if he doesn't realize it, I'll make him aware of the fact," she said to the artificial floral arrangement in the center of the kitchen table.

She smiled, feeling giddy with joy. She realized now that every experience in her life, every hurt, every lonely night had been preparing her for giving herself, heart and soul to Tyler.

Her smile widened. And how like her—to be perverse enough to fall in love with the man she'd once professed to resent and hate with all her being.

After the kitchen was cleaned, she went to the phone and dialed Melissa's number. She wanted her sister to know she'd finally found peace. She also wanted to share the wonder of her love for Tyler.

"How's my little niece or nephew doing today?" Samantha asked when Melissa answered the phone.

"Samantha." Melissa's voice rang with relief. "I think the real question should be how are you doing? I heard some gossip at the store and have been trying to reach you all morning."

"You shouldn't listen to gossip," Samantha replied with a laugh.

"Oh, Sammie, are you really okay? I heard somebody tried to kill you…that Dominic is innocent and the killer came after you last night."

"Hmm, sounds like the local blowhards got it all right. I'm fine, Melissa." For the next few minutes she told Melissa all that had happened with Bones, with Georgia…and finally, with their father and Edie.

"It's all so sad, isn't it?" Melissa said softly when Samantha had finished.

"Yes, it is." Samantha laughed to lighten the mood. "But some things never change. I had the local gossips talking years ago, and I've still got them talking."

Melissa laughed, then sobered. "I'm so glad you're home."

"Me, too." Samantha squeezed the receiver more tightly against her ear. "We've lost too many years, Melissa. But I swear we're going to make up for lost time."

"Yes, I'd like that," her sister answered simply.

Samantha thought about all she'd intended to say to Melissa. She'd intended to tell her sister how much she loved Tyler, but she realized now she wasn't ready to verbalize those feelings. They were still too new, too fresh, too precious to share with anyone other than Tyler. She would tell Melissa later. "I just wanted to call and touch base with you," she finally said. "Tell Bill I said hi and I'll talk to you later."

After hanging up the phone, Samantha curled up in her chair in front of the fire, staring into the flames as visions of a beautiful future unfurled in her mind.

She placed a hand on her stomach, trying to imagine the flutter of life—of Tyler's baby growing inside her.

He would be a wonderful father, just as she knew she would be a good mother. Oh, yes, the Dark residence would once again be filled with the kind of love and laughter she remembered from when her mother had been alive.

The sound of the front door opening jerked her awake, making her realize she'd dozed off. "Tyler?" She jumped up eagerly and met him in the study doorway. "I was beginning to wonder where you'd taken off to."

"The office. I had some loose ends to take care of." He set his briefcase on the floor and walked toward the fire. He held his hands out to the warmth, as if chilled to the bone. He looked tired and Samantha wanted to take him in her arms, pull him against her and soothe the wrinkle furrow in his brow.

"I've been waiting for you to get home. There's something I want to tell you," she said.

He turned to look at her. "I've got something to tell you, too, and I think I'd better go first." He drew in an audible breath and Samantha felt the first stir of unexpected dread. "I'm leaving, Samantha."

The air seemed to whoosh out of her, as if his words were bricks and each had landed on her chest. "Leaving? I don't understand," she finally said, staring at him in confusion. "What do you mean—leaving?"

He raked a hand through his hair, the furrow in his brow deepening. "I'm leaving Wilford…leaving Justice Inc."

Leaving me. The unspoken words echoed in her heart with painful clarity. She sank into the chair, her legs shaking and unable to hold her up. "Tyler…I still don't understand. Why would you want to leave here? I know initially we didn't think a partnership between us would work, but it's worked fine.'' She focused on the business end, at the moment unable to contemplate anything beyond that. ''You can't leave Justice Inc.'' You can't leave me, her heart cried.

Tyler sank into the chair across from her. ''Samantha, from the day you showed up here and learned you were half partner, you've been telling me you won't be happy until I sell out to you. Now you're about to get your wish.''

''I don't want that anymore,'' she cried fervently. ''That was before…that was before I fell in love with you. Tyler, I love you.'' The words jerked out of her as if unwilling to leave and she held her breath, hoping, praying for his response.

''I know,'' he said softly and averted his gaze from her. ''It's probably not really love. You're confused because I was the first man you made love with.''

''Don't tell me what I feel,'' she snapped with a stir of anger. ''Don't cheapen what's in my heart by even thinking such a thing.''

''I'm sorry. You're right, I shouldn't have said that.''

Samantha left her chair and moved to the side of his. She sat on the floor at his feet, staring up at him, the burst of anger gone beneath the weight of confusion.

She knew what she felt for him, but had she mistaken what he felt for her? Had she mistaken his physical attraction for love? Had she misconstrued the expression she sometimes saw in his eyes when he looked at her, the love she felt in his hands when he touched her?

No…she couldn't have. Even now, his love for her radiated from him. She gazed at his face searchingly. ''I know you love me, Tyler. Maybe you don't love me as much as I do you. I know I'm impetuous and difficult. I know that at times I can be a real brat—'' She drew a deep, tremulous breath. "I know I'm not the kind of woman you've probably dreamed about—"

"Dammit, Samantha, stop it." Tyler jerked up out of his chair and pushed past her. He stalked to the doorway, then turned back to her. "Everything is not always about you. This isn't about you. Hell, I love the fact that you're stubborn and impulsive. I even adore you when you're being an utter brat, but I'm not going to stick around to risk my heart again." His features twisted with torment. "I'm a coward, Samantha…and not the kind of man you deserve to have love you." He turned and left the room.

Samantha heard his heavy footsteps as he made his way up the stairs. She felt as if she'd just been kicked in the chest by a mule. A stubborn mule. What was wrong with him? She knew he loved her. He'd said as much. So, why was he denying them their shot at happiness? What was wrong with him?

And what was wrong with her? She shouldn't be just sitting here, letting him walk away from her and her love. She should be upstairs fighting him, making him understand that they belonged together.

She clumped up the stairs, emotional turmoil twisting inside her. He was in his bedroom, a suitcase open on his bed. "What are you doing?" she demanded, the sight of him packing clothes giving his words new weight.

"I've got a plane to catch this evening to St. Louis. First thing tomorrow morning I have a meeting with the people from the firm where I'll be working." He didn't look at her. Instead he moved to the closet, took out a shirt, then walked back to the bed where he carefully folded the piece of clothing and placed it in the suitcase.

"So, you're just going to throw it all away?"

"There's nothing to throw away."

"There's us," she said passionately.

He shook his head. "There is no us."

"Is this about your mother?"

He froze, his eyes darting to hers. "It's about everything. It's about my mother, and Abigail, and your father—it's all about loving and loss."

Samantha walked toward him, wanting to touch him, knowing she had to reach him somehow. His eyes filled with misery as she drew closer...closer still. "Oh, Tyler, love isn't about loss."

He took a step back from her, the misery gone from his eyes, replaced by a dark harshness. "Trust me, Samantha. You don't want to love me. I'm not worth it." His handsome features twisted in agony. "Don't you understand? If it wasn't for me, my mom would still be alive." The words exploded out of him, as if they'd been under pressure and had finally escaped.

Samantha stared at him in surprise. "What are you talking about? You didn't kill your mother."

"I might just as well have.... I blew off my curfew." His hands clenched into fists at his sides. "If I hadn't, I could have stopped him.... I could have changed things."

"Dear God, Tyler. You were just a boy. Had you gotten home any sooner, you might have been killed as well."

He blinked, as if he'd never considered that fact before. He steadied himself with a deep breath and his hands unclenched. "It doesn't matter now," he replied. "It's over and done and I don't ever want to suffer that kind of loss again." He turned to go back to the closet, but Samantha grabbed his arm stopping him.

"Listen to me, Tyler," she said frantically. "I know

all about feeling bad—feeling guilty and believing nobody could ever love me. But you're wrong about yourself." She placed a hand on the side of his face...the beautiful face she loved. "I don't fall in love with unworthy men. I'm not that damned easy."

He jerked away from her, as if he couldn't bear her touch. "And I don't fall in love at all," he said, his voice flat and unemotional.

Samantha watched as he grabbed another shirt from the closet. Her heart pounded with a fearful rhythm. Frantically she searched her mind for a way to reach him, a way to make him understand that they were meant for each other.

"I finally figured out the lesson I think we were supposed to learn from everything that has happened," she said and heard the deep emotion that trembled in her voice. "It's about letting go."

He paused in his folding and looked at her, his eyes a deep navy blue and impossible to read. She sank down on the edge of his bed, knowing this was her last chance to reach the darkness of guilt and fear that resided deep inside him. "If my father had been able to let go of the memory of my mother, then his heart might have reopened to new love and he wouldn't be dead. If Georgia had been able to let go of Morgan, then perhaps Abigail would still be alive."

She leaned forward, wanting him to understand what she was trying to say. "And it wasn't until I let go of my past with my father that my heart opened to the possibility of finding love with you. It's about letting go, Tyler. Letting go of past hurts and lost loves and allowing yourself the hope and openness to live and love again. Let go, Tyler...."

He remained still for what seemed like an eternity.

"That's exactly what I'm doing," he finally said. "I'm letting go of you."

She felt as if she'd been slapped. Any hope she'd had drained from her. She could tell by the sound of his voice, the look in his eyes, that she'd lost him. Before she'd ever really had him.

He continued his packing while she tried to summon the strength to leave the room. She'd been afraid that if she lost the Marcola case, she would somehow lose her soul. She now realized that hadn't been true; Tyler owned her soul along with her heart. And now it wasn't just her heart breaking in two, it was her very soul. Still, she loved him enough to do one last thing, to offer him one last gift of love.

"You don't have to go," she said dully. She stood and walked toward the door. "I'll sell you my half of Justice Inc."

Shock swept over his face. "What?"

"You heard me." She forced a light laugh. "You know me, Tyler. It wouldn't take long before I'd be bored to tears here in Wilford. Justice Inc. was never really mine. It never really belonged to me. It's always been yours. You've worked for it all these years. You deserve it."

"Samantha, I can't let you do that," he protested.

"You aren't letting me do anything. You might just as well buy my half as somebody else. One way or another, I'm selling out." She forced a lightness into her voice. "While you were out today I got a call from a big Chicago firm. They offered me a job and I'm taking it. I'll be much happier at a bigger firm, in a bigger city. I'll draw up the necessary paperwork for the sale." Without waiting for his reply, she turned and left the room.

She fled into her bedroom and closed and locked the door behind her. Now that she'd made the decision, she didn't want to talk about it, didn't want him to try to talk her out of it.

Tyler had put years of his life into Justice Inc. He'd made a sterling reputation for both himself and the firm, carrying on the work her father had begun so many years before. It wasn't fair for him to have to leave it all behind. It was right that she be the one to go. But that didn't make the prospect any easier.

She'd left years ago, filled with burning resentment and a self-destructive anger. Those particular emotions were gone. This time, she would leave with her heart scarred and bereavement weighing heavily upon her.

She realized now the depth of Edie's pain—the pain of shattered dreams and impossible love. Would Edie's pain ever go away? Would her own? She couldn't imagine a time coming when she wouldn't love Tyler. Her love for him flowed within the blood in her veins, whispered in and out with each breath she took.

Walking to the window, she fought the tears that thickened in her throat and burned at her eyes. She knew she should be making plans, figuring out where she would go, what she would do.

Later, she thought. Later she would figure out where she would go. At the moment it was just too painful to consider. At the moment she wanted nothing more than to cry—for Tyler, and for herself, and for all the wonderful things they would never share.

Tyler leaned his head back against the airplane seat. He was exhausted. More than bone weary, he was heartsick. He'd tossed and turned all night, finding sleep impossible. When he'd gotten up that morning he'd found

on the table a sheet of paper outlining the sale of Justice
Inc. to him and he'd realized that Samantha must not
have slept at all either.

Closing his eyes, a vision of Samantha filled his
mind. It was a painful image of her sitting on the edge
of his bed, her eyes filled with tears, with pain.

Dammit, although he'd known the final confrontation
with her would be difficult, he hadn't realized it would
be as heartbreaking as it had been. But he'd done the
right thing, he told himself. She would be better off
without him.

She'd surprised him with her offer to sell out. His
first reaction had been to ignore the offer and follow
through on his plans to join the St. Louis firm. But she'd
made it clear she didn't intend to stick around, planned
to take the Chicago job.

He'd decided to go ahead and fly to St. Louis to tell
Bruno, Sandorf and Kearnes in person that he was de-
clining their job offer. He was going to stay at Justice
Inc.

Even though Samantha was leaving and would no
longer be living in the house, Tyler also realized he
needed to make arrangements to move out.

There was no way he could sit in front of the fire and
not see her image—in that damnably sexy blue silk
robe, curled up in the chair across from him. There was
no way he could sit at the kitchen table and not see her
with her eyes sparkling as she debated with him.

More than anything, there was no way he could sleep
in his bed and not remember the way her hair had
splayed across his navy sheets, how her passionate little
cries had warmed his neck—the very splendor of making love to her.

He would find himself a little studio apartment, a

place with no memories of Samantha. Now, if he could just get those memories out of his head, he would be fine.

As the jet engines began the roar that signaled take-off, Tyler told himself again that he'd done the right thing. Samantha would have a good life in Chicago. She no longer carried the scars from her father's upbringing, and eventually her heart would open to a new love. Yes, he'd done the right thing. So, why did it hurt so badly?

Chapter 16

"It's my landlord. He keeps coming into my apartment when I'm not home." Gina Morris, an attractive eighteen-year-old, sat in front of Samantha's desk, her face flushed with a hint of embarrassment.

"What exactly is it you'd like me to do?" Samantha asked the young woman.

"I just thought maybe you could write a letter, tell him to stop invading my privacy. I mean, he can't do that, can he? Just walk into my place whenever he feels like it?"

Samantha smiled at her reassuringly. "No, he can't. I'll get a letter out this afternoon." Samantha stood and walked Gina to her office door. "You can let Mr. Sinclair know if anything further needs to be done."

"Oh, thank you... I really appreciate it."

Samantha sighed in relief as she closed the door behind Gina. Amazing. It was a few minutes before noon and she'd already seen four prospective clients. Dominic's release had become public news and suddenly Samantha was being regarded as the next Clarence Darrow.

With each person she'd spoken to, she'd explained that she wouldn't be in town long, but would take notes and pass them along to Tyler. And that was exactly what she had done.

Tyler. His name alone caused a shaft of pain to pierce her heart. She'd heard him leave the house that morning, and had found a note when she'd finally gotten out of bed and gone downstairs. The note told her he accepted her terms for sale and had gone to St. Louis to tell the law firm there that he was declining their proffered position.

Finally he'd added that he would be back in a couple of days—time she knew he would take to further distance himself from her emotionally.

Samantha had decided to come into the office, unable to face the prospect of hanging around the house and thinking of Tyler and what might have been. She'd been surprised to see Edie at the receptionist's desk when she arrived.

"I...I didn't know if I should come to work or not," Edie had said tearfully.

Samantha had hugged the older woman. "Of course, you should be here at work."

"Samantha...I never meant—"

"Shh, we won't talk about it again," Samantha had said.

Samantha rose from her desk and looked at her watch. She was meeting Melissa at the club for lunch in a little while and after that, she had to decide where she was going to make her home. Maybe she should contact that St. Louis firm. Since Tyler wasn't taking the job, perhaps she could.

It wasn't a serious thought, however. She'd told Tyler she was going to Chicago, and that was where she would go. She'd never been to the windy city but hoped that there she might heal her wounded heart.

She went over to her window and stared outside, unseeing. At least in Chicago there would be nothing to remind her of Tyler. She frowned. Who was she kidding? There would always be something to evoke memories of him. The blue of the sky would remind her of his eyes. Sooty night shadows would remind her of his hair. Sunset would evoke memories of them making love before the fire, and sunrise would remind her of another day without him.

"Damn him," she said with a sigh. Damn him for being exactly the kind of man he was…and damn him for not being man enough to admit it.

Before tears could fall, before her thoughts could cause her heart to press any more painfully in her chest, she left her office. "I'm going to lunch," she said to Edie. "I'll try to be back by two. If you need me before then, you can call me at the club."

Minutes later, driving toward the club, Samantha focused on the next difficult task she had before her—telling her sister she was leaving town again. But this time it would be different. She didn't intend a self-imposed exile. She wasn't going to ostracize herself from her sister. This time there would be phone calls, and letters and visits. Chicago wasn't so very far away; Samantha could fly back and stay with Melissa and her husband every once in a while. She just hoped Melissa understood why she couldn't remain in Wilford and see Tyler every day.

The hostess led Samantha to the same table where she'd had lunch with Melissa the day after she'd returned to town. Samantha sank into her chair and stared out the window, remembering that at some point in the conversation that day, Melissa had warned her not to hurt Tyler. How ironic, that it had been Tyler who'd inflicted the final killing wounds.

Outside, the day was gray and the sky overcast with gloomy clouds that perfectly reflected Samantha's mood. In the brief time she'd been back in Wilford, she'd found the kind of peace she'd sought so many years before. The place she'd once run from had finally become home, and the thought of leaving tore her apart. But the thought of remaining was absolutely impossible to consider. There was no way she could live in Wilford, see Tyler even in passing, hear the mere mention of his name and not have her heart break a little bit more each time.

"Hey, you're early." Melissa's voice broke into Samantha's thoughts.

She smiled at her sister, who sank into the chair across from her. "How's my niece?"

Melissa laughed and touched her stomach. "Or nephew."

Samantha shook her head. "No, I've decided you need to have a girl. Girls, I understand. Boys, I just don't get."

Melissa's intent gaze examined Samantha's features. "What's happened, Samantha? You look so...lost."

Samantha had been proud of herself. All morning long she'd dealt with people, handled situations and not once had she lost control of her emotions. But Melissa's words made something snap and instantly tears burned in her eyes. She bit the inside of her cheek and swallowed hard to control herself. "I've gone and done something very stupid, Melissa."

Melissa smiled at her fondly. "Now, why doesn't that surprise me? What have you done this time?"

"I've managed to fall hopelessly, desperately in love with Tyler," Samantha confessed.

Melissa clapped her hands together. "But that's wonderful." Her smile faded when Samantha didn't respond in kind. "It's not wonderful?"

Samantha shook her head. "It's impossible, that's what it is." She drew a deep breath, then spilled her heart to Melissa, telling her sister of her love, and Tyler's final rejection of that love. "So, it seems I'm selling my half of the law firm to Tyler and leaving sometime in the near future for a job in Chicago." Deliberately she neglected to add that the job offer from the Chicago firm had been strictly a figment of her imagination. She knew such information would only make Melissa worry.

"Chicago… It seems too far away." Melissa reached across the table and touched Samantha's hand. "I feel like I just found you and now I'm going to lose you again."

Samantha grabbed Melissa's hand. "No way. You aren't about to lose me. I'll fly back here to visit you and your family at least once a month or so…and we'll talk on the phone every day. This isn't going to be like the last time, Melissa. I swear this time will be different."

"And this time I believe you," Melissa replied. Their conversation was interrupted by the waiter. When he'd taken their orders and departed, Melissa sipped her iced tea, then leaned back in her chair with a sigh. "Are you sure you can't stay here in town?"

Samantha hesitated, then shook her head. "One of us has to go, and it's not fair that it be Tyler. He's always belonged here more than I have. This is his home...his work.... I can't take that away from him."

Melissa's gaze was soft, filled with empathy. "Oh Samantha, I don't want you to go, but I'm so proud of the selfless decision you've made. Tyler is the real loser in all this. You would have been good to him...for him."

Samantha raised her chin a notch. "I would have been the best damned wife he'd ever think of having," she said, then burst into tears.

Thankfully, the tears didn't last long, and Samantha managed to control herself for the remainder of the lunch. After saying goodbye to Melissa, she drove to a bookstore that carried out-of-town newspapers. She picked up several days worth of the Chicago *Tribune,* then went back to the office.

"Hold my calls," she told Edie as she breezed in. "I don't want to be disturbed for the next couple of hours." She went into her private sanctum and closed the door.

She didn't want to spend any more time talking to potential clients when she wouldn't be around to do anything with their cases. And she didn't want to put off for another minute finding a place to live...a job. She had to be prepared to leave soon—almost as soon as Tyler returned from his trip.

She couldn't bear the thought of sharing the house with him, seeing him here at work, loving him each and every moment and not having that love returned. It was much too painful to contemplate. She had to be ready to leave...soon.

* * *

Tyler cruised his rental car slowly down the neighborhood street, memory playing games in his mind. Hadn't his best friend, Paul, lived on the corner? When had it become a store? Hadn't the Gerdes twins lived in the building that now housed a fire department? Was it his memory that had failed or had the streets where he'd grown up become unrecognizable?

Of course it wasn't his memory. Nothing ever stayed the same. Except me, Tyler thought. He'd left here an angry young man and had returned with those same feelings boiling inside him.

He frowned thoughtfully. Was Samantha right? Was it all about learning to let go? Finding the peace to start again? He drove slowly, seeing no familiar faces. When he came to the place where the apartment building he'd lived in should have been, he found an empty lot with swing sets and slides. At some point in the passing years, the old brick eight-story building had been razed and replaced with a neighborhood park. He stopped at the curb and rolled down his window. Two little girls sat on swings, looking chubby in their heavy winter coats. Their giggles filled the air as they pumped their legs to make their swings go higher and faster.

To Tyler, the girlish laughter sounded like hope, like new beginnings. It somehow seemed fitting that the place he'd once thought of as a place of death, was now a park where children played, and dreamed, and hoped for the future.

He looked at his watch. He had a two o'clock flight back to Wilford. There was still time, and he had one more stop to make before he said a final goodbye to St. Louis.

It took him only minutes to drive to Chapelwoods Cemetery. He hadn't been here since his mother's funeral. At that time he'd been too angry, too guilt-ridden to properly tell her goodbye.

Just as he'd told Samantha she had to make peace with her father, Tyler knew it was time for him to make peace with his mother.

Unlike Jamison's headstone, which was large and ornate, Kelly Sinclair's was small, a simple concrete square with only her name and the dates she'd been on earth engraved on it. There hadn't been money for anything more elaborate.

Tyler crouched down beside it and gently pulled away dead grass and brushed at fallen leaves. He stared at the dates. She'd been thirty-two when she was killed. So young. And yet, he had a feeling she'd squeezed in more life in those brief years than people who lived to be a hundred. Like Samantha, Kelly Sinclair had embraced each moment as if it was to be her very last. A trait to envy, not fear.

He straightened, realizing that his anger—at fate and at his mother—was gone. Guilt no longer resided inside him. His heart, his very being was filled with one single emotion—his love for Samantha.

It was already too late to shield himself from hurt. He loved Samantha and she loved him, and it didn't matter if she went to Chicago or flew to the moon, he wouldn't feel complete without her.

He'd been afraid, so afraid that she would leave him the way his mother had; but now he realized he would rather have one moment in Samantha's arms than a lifetime of safe aloneness.

He had to get back to Wilford. He had to stop her from taking that Chicago job offer. As he hurried to the car, his mind whirled. It was strange, that offer coming to her on the day after Bones had attacked them. She'd said they'd heard about the Marcola case and had made her the offer. But that was impossible. It had been too soon. There had been no newspaper accounts about what had happened, no way for a law firm in Chicago to know the events that had transpired.

He got back into his car and stared at the dashboard. "She lied." The brat had made the whole thing up and he'd fallen for it, hook, line and sinker. Why? Why would she make up such a thing?

Because she loves you, a small voice replied. She loves you enough to let you have Justice Inc. She loves you enough to sacrifice her father's legacy so you can have what you want. How could he turn his back on that kind of love?

Tyler's throat closed up as he realized the depth of Samantha's love for him. And to think he'd been about to throw it all away. He started the car, hoping, praying that when he got back to Wilford, Samantha would still be there...and would still want him.

"Gary Watters insists on speaking to you," Edie said from Samantha's office doorway.

"Just a few minutes, Samantha," Gary said as he pushed past Edie and slid into the chair across from Samantha's desk.

Samantha looked at her watch. After four. She should be at home packing her bags. She should be doing a thousand things to prepare for leaving. Edie had been fending off reporters all afternoon. Samantha decided she might as well get this over with. Besides, Gary Watters had written a headline Samantha loved: Sexy Samantha Seeks Justice. "Ten minutes," she agreed, then motioned for Edie to close the door.

The reporter took out a notepad and pencil. "Thanks,

Samantha. We've all got the official reports of what happened night before last, but nobody has been able to interview you. This is going be a terrific scoop.''

Samantha smiled at Gary's eagerness. ''If you have the official reports, then you probably have all that you need.''

''No way,'' Gary protested. ''What I want is an actual recounting from you about everything…. How you figured out Georgia Monroe was involved, how you felt when this Bones person tried to attack you. And I want to know what made you defend Dominic Marcola when most everyone in town thought he was guilty as sin.''

Before Samantha could answer, the door to her office burst open. Tyler stepped in. ''Get out, Watters. I need to speak with my partner,'' he said.

''Stay here, Gary,'' Samantha countered. ''Mr. Sinclair has nothing to say to me that I want to hear.'' Damn him, she thought. What was he doing back here so soon? Why did he have to look so damned handsome? Why hadn't he stayed in St. Louis until she'd left Wilford so she would never have to see him again?

Gary looked from one to the other, not rising from his seat.

''You lied to me, Samantha,'' Tyler accused. ''You lied about the Chicago job offer.''

She felt the heat of a flush sweep over her face. ''Tyler, this really isn't the proper time to discuss it. Gary is in the middle of interviewing me.''

''You're telling me what's proper and what's not?'' Tyler threw back his head and laughed. ''That's rich, but at the moment I don't give a damn about proper behavior. I'm feeling decidedly improper.'' He advanced toward her desk.

Samantha jumped up, uneasy about the fiery light she

saw in Tyler's eyes. Had she somehow managed to drive him over the edge of sanity? God knew, he'd told her often enough she would drive him crazy. She stepped away from him, stopping only when her back hit the wall.

"Tell me why you lied, Samantha." He braced an arm on either side of her, effectively making it impossible for Samantha to go anywhere. "Why did you lie?" he demanded softly, his breath warm on her face.

"Tyler..." she said between clenched teeth, motioning toward Gary, who took notes furiously, a huge grin on his face. "Have you gone crazy?" She tried to duck out from under, but he tightened his arms, holding her captive.

"Talk to me, Samantha," he persisted.

Samantha shot another look at Gary, who seemed to be enjoying the action, then looked at Tyler helplessly. "What do you want, Tyler? You want to hear me say it again? You want to know just how much I love you? All right, I'll tell you. I love you more than anything I've ever loved before. That's why I lied about the job in Chicago. Even though you don't want me, I love you enough not to take Justice Inc. from you."

To her horror, tears sprang to her eyes. "I love you enough to go away and let you live your life in peace." She swiped at her tears, angry that he seemed bent on humiliating her. "Dammit, Gary, would you please leave?" she begged.

"Don't you leave that chair," Tyler said to the reporter. "It would be far too predictable for me to ask you to leave. Just to show my own brand of perverseness, I want you to stay and listen while I propose."

"Propose?" Samantha stared at him in surprise.

"Hot damn!" Gary exclaimed.

"Propose what?" Samantha demanded with narrowed eyes. She was afraid to hope, afraid to believe her dreams might actually have a shot at coming true.

"Marriage, what else?" Tyler drew her into his arms, his eyes lit with a glow that stole her breath away. "Marry me, Samantha. Be my partner…be my wife."

Samantha's heart beat rapidly at his words, at the future they promised. Still, she held down her joy, refusing to allow its complete release. She didn't doubt her own feelings where he was concerned, but she needed to make absolutely certain about his. "Yesterday you didn't even think we could be partners in the firm. Now you're asking me to be your life partner. What changed?"

Tyler took his hands and framed her face, his gaze so filled with love she felt it penetrate through her, touching her heart with warmth. "Nothing changed…and everything changed. I went to my mother's grave, and I realized that I've been afraid to love you because I thought you'd die like she did—too soon."

Samantha shook her head. "I don't intend on going anywhere for a very long time."

"It doesn't matter anyway." He caressed her cheeks with his thumbs. "Whatever time there is, I want to spend it with you, whether it's a moment, an hour…or years. Oh, Samantha, I was a fool to turn my back on your love. Tell me it's not too late. Tell me you'll marry me."

"Yes…yes, I'll marry you." She barely got the words out when his lips captured hers in a kiss that spoke all the things she needed to hear, all the promises to last a lifetime.

He drew back from her, a smile curving his lips.

"We're going to fill that house with children and with love. You'll be one hell of a mother."

She smiled tremulously. "I'll make you one hell of a wife," she promised.

"This is going to be one hell of a story," Gary exclaimed from behind them. Samantha jumped in surprise. She'd forgotten all about the reporter's presence.

"Get out, Gary," Tyler said, the look in his eyes sending shivers of anticipatory delight through Samantha.

"Yeah, Gary…get out," she echoed.

"Yes, but the story—"

"Out!" Tyler and Samantha yelled it together. Gary jumped out of his chair and scooted toward the door.

When he was gone, Tyler turned back to Samantha, his arms tightening around her, drawing her intimately close against him. "Now…where were we?" He smiled, the light in his eyes fiery with desire.

"You were telling me how much you love me, how you can't live without me," Samantha replied.

He nodded, the glint of humor gone from his eyes as he looked at her intently. "I could live without you, Samantha, if I had to…but it wouldn't be living, it would simply be surviving. I've done that for too long. Closed myself off emotionally, held on to the pain of the past for too long."

Samantha traced the line of his brow with a fingertip. She knew all about emotional pain, and somehow she believed that fate had brought them together to heal each other. "I think we were destined to be together from the moment my father brought you home that first time."

He smiled, with no shadows in his eyes, only love.

"And I think I fell in love with you that night I hauled you out of that bar and you tried to seduce me."

"You should have let me seduce you that night. Just think of all the time we've wasted."

He laughed. "I'm all for not wasting another minute. Tell me, if I were to make love to my fiancée right here in this office...would that be unpredictable?"

She nodded, leaning her head back as he trailed blazing kisses along the column of her neck. "It would be utterly scandalous."

"Oh, my love, I can't think of anyone I'd rather be scandalous with," he told her. With one smooth movement, he picked her up and carried her to the love seat.

"You're beginning to show real promise, Sinclair," Samantha said softly.

He laughed and stroked a finger down her cheek, loving her with his eyes, with his touch. "I'm just getting started, my love."

As his mouth touched hers again, Samantha tasted the promise of their future on his lips—a future filled with laughter and challenge—but more than anything, with love forever and ever.

* * * * *

Take 4 bestselling love stories FREE

Plus get a FREE surprise gift!

Special Limited-time Offer

Mail to Silhouette Reader Service™

3010 Walden Avenue
P.O. Box 1867
Buffalo, N.Y. 14240-1867

YES! Please send me 4 free Silhouette Intimate Moments® novels and my free surprise gift. Then send me 6 brand-new novels every month, which I will receive months before they appear in bookstores. Bill me at the low price of $3.57 each plus 25¢ delivery and applicable sales tax, if any.* That's the complete price and a savings of over 10% off the cover prices—quite a bargain! I understand that accepting the books and gift places me under no obligation ever to buy any books. I can always return a shipment and cancel at any time. Even if I never buy another book from Silhouette, the 4 free books and the surprise gift are mine to keep forever.

245 SEN CF2V

Name _____ (PLEASE PRINT)

Address _____ Apt. No. _____

City _____ State _____ Zip _____

This offer is limited to one order per household and not valid to present Silhouette Intimate Moments® subscribers. *Terms and prices are subject to change without notice. Sales tax applicable in N.Y.

UMOM-696   ©1990 Harlequin Enterprises Limited

ALL THAT GLITTERS

by *New York Times* bestselling author

LINDA HOWARD

Greek billionaire Nikolas Constantinos was used to getting what he wanted—in business and in his personal life. Until he met Jessica Stanton. Love hadn't been part of his plan. But love was the one thing he couldn't control.

From *New York Times* bestselling author Linda Howard comes a sensual tale of business and pleasure—of a man who wants both and a woman who wants more.

BEVERLY BARTON

Continues the twelve-book series— 36 Hours—in April 1998 with Book Ten

NINE MONTHS

Paige Summers couldn't have been more shocked when she learned that the man with whom she had spent one passionate, stormy night was none other than her arrogant new boss! And just because he was the father of her unborn baby didn't give him the right to claim her as his wife. Especially when he wasn't offering the one thing she wanted: his heart.

For Jared and Paige and *all* the residents of Grand Springs, Colorado, the storm-induced blackout was just the beginning of 36 Hours that changed *everything!* You won't want to miss a single book.

Available at your favorite retail outlet.

DIANA PALMER
ANN MAJOR
SUSAN MALLERY

RETURN TO WHITEHORN

In **April 1998** get ready to catch the bouquet. Join in the excitement as these bestselling authors lead us down the aisle with three heartwarming tales of love and matrimony in Big Sky country.

A very engaged lady is having second thoughts about her intended; a pregnant librarian is wooed by the town bad boy; a cowgirl meets up with her first love. Which Maverick will be the next one to get hitched?

Available in **April 1998.**

Silhouette's beloved **MONTANA MAVERICKS** returns in Special Edition and Harlequin Historicals starting in February 1998, with brand-new stories from your favorite authors.

Round up these great new stories at your favorite retail outlet.

PSMMWEDS